Other titles by the author:

When Charlotte Comes Home

The Enigma of Iris Murphy:
Stories

Maureen Millea Smith

Livingston Press

at

The University of West Alabama

Typesetting and page layout: Teresa Boykin, Ciara Denson
Proofreading: Maggie Slimp, Jessie Hagler, Joe Taylor
Cover art and design: Steve Smith
Cover layout: Sofia Rodas

For my sister, Megan Frances Millea,

in Charlotte, North Carolina

This is a work of fiction.
Surely you know the rest: any resemblance
to persons living or dead is coincidental.

Livingston Press is part of The University of West Alabama,
and thereby has non-profit status.
Donations are tax-deductible:
brothers and sisters, we need 'em.

first edition
6 5 4 3 3 2 1

The Enigma of Iris Murphy: Stories

Table of Contents

"We are all anxious to be understood, and it is very hard not to be. But there is one thing much more necessary."

"What is that grandmother?"

"To understand other people."

—*The Princess and the Goblin*

George MacDonald

Pardon Palimpsest

THEY SMELL IRIS MURPHY BEFORE THEY SEE HER.

She wears a faint scent that could best be described as clean and comforting and probably expensive and not sold at Target. Or at least this is how Kenneth Yellow Dog has always thought of her perfume. It wafts into the visitation area of the Nebraska State Penitentiary in Lincoln announcing her. The convicted and their guests pause to inhale, momentarily stopping their conversations. Seconds later when she walks into the room heads turn.

"The Bird, The Bird," they say in astonishment to one another.

The convicts all know that this is a rare sighting. Rumor has it, that she is afraid of prisons and that bars and razor wire send her into panic attacks. What they know about Iris Murphy is what they've heard about her. Some somebody telling another somebody a story that another guy's cousin swears to be the truth about this public defender. They believe it, though. For them it is immutable, a fact, a law of the physics that defines the gravity of their world. In this way, as in many ways, felons are like all other human beings. Their beliefs are based on stories.

When a visitor shouts out,

"Hey, Ms. Murphy!"

This draws a wary prison guard's attention.

"You know the rules, keep to your own conversation," he barks in warning at the speaker and to everyone else in the room. "This ain't the neighborhood."

When the guard looks away Iris Murphy greets the offending voice with a slight nod of her head and a small wave. The woman smiles back at Ms. Murphy and then gives the uniformed man's back the stink-eye, before returning to the story she was telling about a cousin and a baby. The listener is her boyfriend, a once bungling burglar who decided to kiss a sleeping teenage girl, rather than just steal the cash he had found in her parents' bedroom. She awakened and screamed before hitting him. He then did her unforgettable harm. Now he is a rapist. His girl-friend blames it on the methamphetamines.

With a slight twist of his neck, Kenneth watches the scene unfold. He knows Iris Murphy to be rare and good, beautiful and generous, and inscrutable. Dressed in a tailored pink suit and pearls she appears to have stepped out of a time machine, a woman of 1956, or 1961, who has materialized into late April of 2012. He knows that her patent leath-er pumps are undoubtedly Italian in origin and that she has chosen a wine-colored lipstick in a matte finish because it brings out the contrast in her pale skin and silver hair.

"I would fade away without the lipstick, Kenneth," Iris once told him. He was walking her to her car after a Democratic Party meeting.

Ms. Murphy's style does not matter to the felons. What matters to them is her ethic. After over thirty years at the Douglas County Public Defender's Office in Omaha, Ms. Murphy still works hard. She doesn't lecture her clients. She knows everyone at the Courthouse, and she knows what to plead and who to cajole. Her manners are impeccable. She treats homeless men and political wives with the same kind courtesy. Before judges she wears conservative suits tailored to please them. Cops call her "The Bird." It is an apt comment of disrespect referring to the plumage of her clothes outside of the Douglas County Courthouse where she dresses like Audrey Hepburn or Jacqueline Kennedy and never Mar-ilyn Monroe.

An ex-con can see Ms. Murphy from a distance on Farnam Street, or in the Old Market, wearing a Pucci dress or a Chanel suit. (Kenneth knows this because he saw Iris Murphy long before he met her.) No felon, however, will ever care about the provenance of Iris's clothing. For they dress in jeans, T-shirts, and basketball shoes all bought at Walmart, or in a thrift store. If they aspire to something better, and probably some of them do, they will never announce it. An eye toward style would be considered different, almost queer, and perception is everything to them. What they like is the pop of the color in Ms. Murphy's threads and that she's pretty, even if she's old. For them her beauty feels like an act of defiance. She doesn't care about what the cops think of her, or her clothing, and not caring is basically the convict's credo. The very sight of her breeds hope in their hearts, that thing of feathers. So for the felons, Ms. Murphy is "The Bird" as well.

There is a collective intake of breath among those in the room when Iris Murphy sits down with the deaf-mute Leonard Howard and her hands begin to fly. The inmates know that Leonard Howard was never a client of the public defender's office. He is a man who still has money and whose attorney is one of his rare visitors. A little boy tugs on a woman's hoodie, saying,

"They're talking with their hands, Grandma."

The boy's grandmother ignores him, as do the guards, because they are trying to translate what the hands are saying while pretending not to pay attention even as they speak. (The guards allow for the rumble of one-on-one conversations. It is the call and response, the groupthink of it that they halt and despise.) None of them have the faintest idea of how Ms. Murphy could know Leonard Howard. Collectively it feels wrong to the felons and their visitors, for they believe that she is theirs. Information has been withheld from them and they will get to the bottom of this breach in due course.

This meeting does not surprise Kenneth Yellow Dog. Iris Murphy has a profoundly deaf sister who lives in Cincinnati. He met the sister years ago when he ran into Iris and her family at the zoo. The deaf community in Nebraska is small and insular by the very nature of the disability, so Iris would know Leonard. However, seeing Iris and Leonard together does create a knot of worry in Kenneth's stomach. He shares a cell with Leonard Howard. Leonard is a man of issues that have nothing to do with his deafness. When Leonard is in the mood to talk about them, he writes in a small notebook that he keeps in his shirt pocket, ripping out page after page to hand off to Kenneth in his manic moments. Leonard's political views, his misogyny, and his desire to register on free Internet dating sites once he is released from prison are topics he has addressed in his near perfect cursive. When Leonard feels less agitated about the world he teaches American Sign Language to Kenneth, and Kenneth has been happy to learn what he can. A commitment to learning something everyday is part of the habit of his life, in or outside of incarceration.

Kenneth adjusts his eyes, bringing his attention back to his own visitor. He sits across from his cousin the attorney, Cameron Kills Pretty Enemy. The two men sit on molded plastic chairs the color of blueberries. The chairs are armless. Between them is a small round-topped table that reaches their shins. There is something of a contemporary art center feel to the room's design, but also a sense of a military recruiter's office in a poor neighborhood's strip mall. Kenneth realizes the didactic purpose of the scene every Thursday. Thursday is his day for visits. Once a month Cameron drives the seven hours from Prior Lake, Minnesota to see him while Kenneth's colleague Alfred Moorman comes on an alternate Thursday to report on the Willa Cather Branch Library in Omaha. This is the library that Kenneth has managed for seven years and from which he has taken a formal leave to serve out his prison sentence. Whether he will be reinstated as manager there is up to the library director and the Mayor of Omaha. Kenneth's fiancée, Madeline Rea, visits on the other two Thursdays.

Beyond Iris Murphy and Leonard Howard, Kenneth can see men with women and children and a few men with men in the periphery of his vision. Their chorus of conversations creates a constant background noise that mutes individual exchanges. It is hoped that visits will promote a sense of support from family and that the very controlled nature of the room will create a template of bonds not based on drama or drugs. Kenneth did vast amounts of research on prison life before surrendering himself in Lincoln. He prepared, as best he could, before arriving for his nineteen-month sentence and he understands the details of his surroundings.

While incarcerated, Kenneth has found it helpful to imagine himself, and each of his fellow prisoners, to be a dog. He is a mastiff among black mouth curs, pit bull mixes, rottweilers, and golden doodles gone wrong. These are the kinds of dogs that turn up at the Nebraska Humane Society where Kenneth has volunteered for many years. They have, at the very least, been neglected, sometimes abused, either by their owners or other dogs, and in general have bad manners, and at their worst are aggressive and dangerous. Many have been abandoned, and an animal control officer will have captured them after a complaint about a dog running loose in an Omaha neighborhood. From there they are delivered to a shelter. Abandoned dogs are manageable, but they are not easy, and often have vast amount of trust issues, making them difficult for people to adopt.

In the population of the Humane Society there are also animals that have been given up by their owners. Since the financial downturn in 2008, people have surrendered animals in record numbers to shelters. These animals come with names, histories, bowls, beds, collars, and tears. Often they are older creatures, white faced and long in tooth, needing love and care, but still very viable. Frankly, it is hard to convince a young family to adopt an older or abandoned animal. They want puppies, kittens, and bunnies, sweet, loveable, and undamaged.

Kenneth assumes that many of his fellow inmates have histories that are similar to those of the abandoned animals. Inevitably these dogs are mixed breeds. They have been trained to defend and fight and have been maltreated for their efforts. The males have gonads the size of small oranges. The bitches are skeletal from too many litters and not enough food. The Humane Society canines talked to Kenneth Yellow Dog like the inmates talk to him here. The dogs told him their stories — the cruel owners, the willing bitches — while prisoners offer up to Kenneth particular chapters of their histories, the better parts of themselves. Unbidden they will hint at why they did what they did and how that brought them to Lincoln. The convicts want the big, quiet Indian on their side, as they do Iris Murphy.

"About the pardon," Cameron says in a very low voice that forces Kenneth to lean into him. "The Board of Pardons meets every six to eight weeks. Your hearing for a pardon, though, won't come until the next quarter."

"Cameron, I want to vote in November."

"Well, I'm sure the Board of Pardons would rather have you not voting in November."

"I didn't hurt anyone. I didn't make any money. I didn't sell drugs. They were just three miniature animals."

"Yeah, but you upset the zoo and you angered the Nebraska Cattlemen's Association."

"I didn't steal cattle."

"Well, little horses are close enough for the Cattlemen. To them it's all cattle. Some of them still think that people should be hung for stealing steers."

"One was a donkey."

"Yeah, but the donkey was the most popular animal of the three."

"I always vote," Kenneth says in a low voice, looking at Cameron and, for a second, across the room at Iris Murphy, a fellow Douglas County Democrat.

"The State of Nebraska will let you be reinstated as a voter two years after your release, with or without a pardon."

"I'm not a felon."

"No one made you die on this sword, Kenneth. You didn't have to take the fall. It's a minor felony, but a felony nonetheless, and so until we can arrange a pardon, you're a felon. The Board has the power to give pardons. Power is about opacity. There are layers to this that must be peeled back, carefully. It is not like an onion."

Kenneth pauses. He is sorely disappointed in this turn of events. He wants to vote again for Barack Obama in November. Kenneth has voted in every election, local and national, since his eighteenth birthday.

Even before he made his plea, his attorney mentioned the possibility of a pardon.

"You'll get pardoned, Kenneth. The Board of Pardons loves to pardon the good guys. You know, the ones who shouldn't have been sentenced in the first place. But mostly, they pardon prominent assholes with tax and fraud convictions."

Inwardly, he sighs and then embraces the vast silence that will compose most of his visitation time with his cousin. Cameron provides presence and the sustaining public notion that he is concerned about his cousin, because he is, even if he doesn't have a lot to say. Prisoners and their guests gape at Cameron Kills Pretty Enemy whenever he walks into the space. He is twenty years older and two inches taller than Kenneth, and that makes him very tall. Cameron wears Tony Lama boots with well-tailored suits. His hair is a long white braid wrapped in a beaded cover. "Indian lawyer," the convicts say under their breath with awe when he passes by.

It is hard for the two cousins to hold an extended conversation because Cameron is not a big talker while Kenneth's talent in life is listening. They are private men. If they have an important concern they keep it to themselves, or tell it to their dog. The give and take of conversation is not part of their friendship. They like being together, plain and simple. Mutual silence is comforting to them.

Kenneth knows that people in the Twin Cities bring problems to Cameron Kills Pretty Enemy — petty crimes, drunken driving arrests, divorce — they pay him to find the least painful of legal answers. Like any attorney, Cameron likes to be paid for both listening and any talking he might do. His net worth has been built on billable hours.

"What about justice?" Kenneth remembers once asking Cameron.

Cameron was working then as a Hennepin County attorney in Minneapolis and Kenneth was a teenager.

"I don't truck in justice."

"What about innocence?"

"There's very little of that in this world."

Even as a teenager Kenneth disagreed with Cameron about his view of the world, but rarely did he challenge his cousin's point-of-view. It was a waste of breath.

But that day in Minneapolis, Kenneth's face must have betrayed him, because Cameron laughed and said, "Kenneth, you're a gosh-darn liberal. You're a soft-hearted man."

Kenneth remembers saying, "I am."

This made Cameron laugh all the more.

Of course, Iris Murphy believes in working for justice.

"Everyone in America likes to think that they did it all on their own. That they jumped out of their mother's womb fully formed, ready to take on the world. They forget that we all come into this world helpless and leave it the same way."

Kenneth can remember hearing Iris say this in late 1999, at a wine and cheese event to raise money for some shared political cause, and his heart beat faster listening to her. It was an odd time for him. His girlfriend had recently broken up with him and moved to Houston. Everyone was worried about computer systems failing at the turn of the new century and millennium. In 1999, the universe seemed to be against Kenneth Yellow Dog, but Iris Murphy never was. She greeted him with a smile every time she saw him that year, and he was a man in need of some smiles.

Kenneth thought 2000 would be better and he worked the phones hard for Al Gore. But Florida, a state he rarely thought about, put his efforts into jeopardy. Chads and Katherine Harris upended everything. During a brief telephone conversation after the election, Cameron had declared, "that there was no difference between Bush and Gore anyway."

"I don't believe that to be true, Cameron," is all Kenneth would say to his cousin, not wanting to argue. Cameron had recently lost his dog, a beautiful golden retriever named Tribulation, and his heart had hardened in grief. Kenneth knew he could not move that stone heart one inch. Cameron concluded the call with these words,

"You know, I'm a Libertarian, these days."

It's what everyone said in 2000, as they held their collective breaths after the election. When the Supreme Court made its decision in December, many people announced that they were Libertarians, implying it would seem, that they had voted for Governor George W. Bush. If politics had taught Kenneth Yellow Dog anything it is that people like to attach themselves to winners. What he knew, as a dependable Democrat, is that people lie about their voting records as much as they do their sex lives.

"The Supreme Court has made a moral error of seismic proportions," Iris Murphy told Kenneth the evening after the Court's announcement. They were leaving a Douglas County Democratic Party gathering.

Kenneth had needed to hear these words from Iris because he believed them to be true, and he knew that most Nebraskans were going to bed happy to have Governor Bush moving into the White House. Many of his patrons were going to walk into the Willa Cather Branch Library relieved by the decision. For days he was going to have to listen to their glee in professional neutrality, privately soldiering on in his minority positions.

By the time they reached her Subaru Forester parked four blocks away on a side street, Kenneth wanted to believe himself to be in love with Iris Murphy. Like-minded politics in an election year can have this effect on people. Furthermore he had always been attracted to Iris, even though she was much older than he. So Kenneth bent down, kissing her full on the lips. What startled him was that tiny Iris kissed him back, opening her mouth and finding his tongue. There in the cold December darkness the tall man and the small woman made out until the headlights of a car turned down the street, forcing them to pull back.

"Iris."

"Kenneth."

She smiled. Her eyes were sparkling, and he felt hope for the first time in weeks. The car passed them by. Then they both laughed, and he kissed her again before she pushed him away to reach into her handbag for her car keys.

Kenneth took her gloved hand, stopping her.

"Marry me, Iris."

"Kenneth!"

"I mean it."

(He remembers sort of meaning it: wanting to sleep with Iris Murphy felt to him, then, like something that should be sanctified by marriage.)

Then she kissed him, her small frame pushing into his crotch, causing a huge erection.

Car lights again illuminated the street and they stepped away from each other.

"Dear Kenneth, I'm way too old for you. You'll want babies. I have hot flashes and elderly parents and a teenage son."

"I love you. We talk. We agree."

"Thank you."

"I do."

"You remind me of a man that I once loved. Kissing you was a gift. It brought back memories, but I'm not the woman you want to spend the rest of your life with."

Kenneth shook his head.

Iris sighed and smiled.

"It's true. I'm an age that I would never tell you. In twenty-four months, you won't be in love with me, but I would still be in love with you. Believe me, I know me. My heart will be broken and you, quite wisely, will be onto the next chapter. I can sense the ending even as I lust after you here on this cold street."

Kenneth dropped her hand, letting Iris fish the Subaru's key out of her purse. Then he kissed her a final time before she drove off to pick up her son. He thinks of all this as Cameron leans into him to say,

"Madeline called me yesterday. The mayor and the library director are going to ask you back. There will be some conditions, but nothing to worry about."

Kenneth can feel his tears.

"Thank you, Cameron."

"A man needs good news."

And then they fall back into their silence amidst chatter and the sound of Leonard Howard's demonstrative and noisy hands. Kenneth's thoughts turn to Madeline Rea, happy that Iris Murphy had not let him pursue her. Two weeks into the new millennium Madeline came to work at the library and Kenneth fell under her spell. Tall and thoughtful, the child of Quakers, twenty-six-year-old Madeline pulled Kenneth into her orbit with kindness. That April, Kenneth took her to the zoo and then to a jazz concert at the Joslyn Art Museum. He gave her a ride home from a library board meeting in May. Each time there was an opportunity for a kiss, but he was afraid of rejection. She was so young and beautiful. Kenneth worried about being too old for her at thirty-eight. In June, when Madeline invited him to her apartment for dinner he arrived with a dozen red roses and condoms in his pocket.

"Kenneth, they're beautiful," she said as he handed her the bouquet. Then she threw her arms around him and kissed him. Once his lips met hers, Kenneth lost all of his reserve. Their tall bodies filled the frame of the doorway. When two cats began to yammer wildly suggestive things to the couple from the safety of a perch in the living room, Kenneth danced Madeline into the apartment, closing the door with his boot. There they stood smooching and exploring each other to the cheering of her felines. When Madeline stepped back from Kenneth to take the roses into the kitchen her wrap dress parted, leaving Kenneth Yellow Dog with his first glimpse of her substantial breasts in a La Perla brassiere. Smiling, she led him past the dining room table that had been set for dinner into the small kitchen.

Madeline put the roses into a vase and turned down the oven. All the while, Kenneth kissed her neck. Then she led him into her bedroom, shutting the door to a chorus of meows, calling out, "Do it, do it, do it." Indeed they did.

It is not a wise thing to think too much about sex in prison. Kenneth misses it terribly. He longs for Madeline. They are going to be married in July, two weeks after his release. Theirs has been a long and pleasurable courtship, until now. He rues their caution. Time always felt like it was on their side. Now he wants a baby, something to lead him forward from these sad days. Like a cat, Kenneth pretends an indifference to his situation that he does not feel. He will not reveal the crushing blow that has been dealt to his spirit in the dark loneliness of this place. Revelation, he fears, would break him.

Then Kenneth looks up to see Cameron's eyes bearing down on Iris Murphy, and he turns his attention to her as well. Iris's hands are flying while her shoulders look stiff, too close to her ears. He notices how thin her arms are as they pull in and out of her three-quarter length sleeves in response to Leonard Howard's emphatic signs. She is a small woman who has grown smaller in the months since Kenneth has been in prison. He considers again the gentle physics of how he would have made love to such a slight human being. It is a challenge he would have taken in a heartbeat that cold December night, or any time Iris could have escaped her responsibilities, and he is glad that she stopped him. Then his thoughts return to Madeline who matches him in so many ways and he thinks this as he watches Cameron begin to flick his fingers in and out of his palms as Cameron stares at Iris Murphy. The thing with his fingers is his cousin's nervous tic, his anxiety made visible. Then Cameron says,

"You and Madeline should have children, Kenneth. I was thinking this just the other day while I was working with our intern, Erma Charging. You would like a daughter like Erma. She is such a sensitive girl. Children lead us forward. They're our future."

Kenneth nods his head and in doing so realizes that Cameron is past middle age. He can hear the crackle of Cameron's knees when he stands up. His cousin's salt and pepper hair is now almost white.

The five-minute warning sounds, announcing that the visitation hour is almost over. Conversations take on speed, get louder, or they lower themselves into a whisper filled with secrets. Men lean into their lovers or wives. They pull their squirming children onto their laps.

Kenneth watches as Leonard Howard pushes his chair back and it scrapes loudly against the industrial linoleum as he stands. Heads turn to observe. Leonard signs something to Iris Murphy that makes her visibly wince. Her eyes blink. The whole room pauses, as a tear runs down her cheek. Leonard looks at Iris without sympathy and then he turns and leaves.

"Please, Leonard," she says and signs to his back

Twice, she brings her small arm to the pink weave of cloth that covers her chest, her fist beating the breast. She breathes deeply before standing up. Then she turns, walking through the phalanx of chairs and bodies her eyes straight ahead on the exit.

"Iris," Kenneth says aloud.

His arm leaves his knee with the intention of reaching out to her. She is within his grasp, but he is stopped by Cameron's hand. Iris Murphy keeps walking as if she does not see the two Lakota men. They are the tallest men in the room and Kenneth knows that they cannot be missed. Even eye contact with her would have reassured him. On this particular day he does not need the Iris Murphy smile, just her recognition. Kenneth is shaken.

"Iris."

Kenneth cannot help repeating her name as she disappears through the doorway.

"Keep to your own conversations," the guard says in warning.

"She's my friend," Kenneth whispers to Cameron. "I want to help her."

"There's nothing you can do for her now," Cameron says in his quiet voice. "I'll speak to her in the parking lot."

"But you don't even know her."

"I know Iris Murphy."

"But how?"

Cameron meets his question with silence as he releases Kenneth's arm. Then time is called and Kenneth stands up and Cameron follows his lead. The two men shake hands and each turns. Kenneth files into the line returning to confinement. Someone farts. The air turns acrid.

From behind him Kenneth hears, "The Big Indian knows The Bird," but he does not look at the speaker. He recognizes the voice. It

Pardon Palimpsest

is a small guy with the nervous nature of a lap dog. He did something stupid with a gun, as jumpy people often do.

Instead, Kenneth Yellow Dog straightens his spine and lowers his shoulders, setting his feet wide. The prisoners give him room.

Property
Crime

Monday mornings are always full of crap. This Sergeant Clayton Santos-Anderson believes to be a universal truth in the world of policing and in life. He thinks this less than positive thought while shutting the door of his truck in the parking lot of the Omaha Police Department. Standing beside his F150, Clayton pauses to study the voice-mail icon on his BlackBerry before activating the device. Sunday night is an incubator of voice-mail, a passive aggressive form of dropping the ball of a problem into someone else's lap. From the tiny speaker in the hand-size rectangle of the glittering device, his ex-wife, Darla, shrieks into his ear about an unpaid housing bill at the University of Nebraska. This is followed by a tearful message from his daughter, Maria, who, unbeknownst to her parents, spent the money that her father had sent to her for room and board on a spring break trip to Padre Island. Someone from the mayor's office called in the middle of the night to request a presentation on property crime to a group in South Omaha. Next there is a pause, a hesitation before he listens to Spanish-inflected words that crash into his heart,

"I love you, Clayton. When are you coming home?"

Yolanda Santos-Anderson's message is loud and short. His mom has always spoken into telephone receivers as though they are orange juice cans attached to taunt strings. At forty-nine-years of age Clayton still misses his mother. When he misses her, he misses Saint Paul and

Mendota Heights where he grew up. He loves the Twins and ice hockey and the progressive state government of his boyhood and then, for a moment, Clayton experiences the twinges of guilt that he always feels when he longs for Saint Paul, because he also loves Omaha, the city he serves. It is a fact that after forty-eight hours of being in Minnesota Clayton will begin to long for his daughter, Maria. This will lead to trying to remember if he watered the plants in his apartment and wondering if Maria will drop by while he is gone to sleep in the pink bedroom that he has maintained for her since the divorce. The seeds of adult homesickness are then planted. By the time he drives over to his brother's place on Prior Lake, Clayton's longing will grow for his friendships in the Omaha Police Department and the slow-pitch softball team that he has captained for twenty years. His mother's words make him feel cloudy with emotion until he listens to a message from a homicide lieutenant, who Clayton knows to be a useless prick except when staring at a murder scene, about a broken window and a pile of dog shit in the Dundee neighborhood of the city that involves a public defender.

Clayton Santos-Anderson has no warm and fuzzy feelings for public defenders, or lawyers in general. His time in the family law courtrooms of the Douglas County Court system has taught him that a lawyer works only when he or she is paid up front and paid well. This has also taught Clayton another universal truth; family law is where the courts see good people at their very worst. Divorce is never pretty. It is like a bad business break up with tragic emotions. Clayton did not break up his marriage, but Darla's affair did not stop Darla from blaming everything on him.

"You live for your career, Clayton," Darla screamed at him when he unexpectedly returned to their home in Millard on his lunch hour to retrieve the wallet that he had forgotten earlier that morning. "You don't even see me."

"I can see you now," is all he could think to say in response to her.

Then he walked far enough into the bedroom to retrieve the wallet from the top drawer of his bureau. After that he turned around, leaving the room and the house, without looking back. Driving downtown to his cubicle at police headquarters, Clayton ate the tuna salad sandwich that Darla had made for him that morning and bawled like a baby.

What Clayton saw in his marital bed was Darla spread eagle beneath a tow-headed and quite buff young man. From the CD player on the bookcase next to the closet, Keane's *Hopes and Fears* wailed. Clayton had given Darla the CD for her birthday three months earlier; it was a big seller in 2004. The white shirt, black tie, and black pants of a Mormon missionary were draped across the rocking chair in the bedroom's far corner. The missionary looked terrified. Darla looked caught.

By the time that Clayton walked out of the garage he knew that his marriage was over. The pain of it was that even standing next to his truck on the asphalt driveway, shaking from shock and rage, his fingertips brushing the holster of his service revolver, he still loved Darla, as fractious, loud and demanding as she was then, and continues to be with him. Hearing Darla's angered voice coming through his BlackBerry reminds him of the energy that attracted him to her in the first place. Her spark could always light his candle. Divorce never stripped Clayton Santos-Anderson of his thankfulness for the better years of their marriage and his eternal gratitude for Maria. They did go to marriage counseling, but Darla blamed her infidelity on Clayton's work as a police officer.

"There's never enough money," Darla said. "We can't even go to fucking Lake Okoboji."

"If you two saved the money and planned the vacation, then how would that make you feel?" the therapist asked Darla.

"I don't want to go to Okoboji," Darla said. "I mean, really, I would rather go to Hawaii, but a police sergeant could never afford Hawaii."

"But if you two could go to Hawaii, just suppose, how would you feel then?"

"You always side with Clayton," Darla said, giving the therapist the stink eye. "You think I'm a slut because I slept with Jacob."

"Darla, I love you," Clayton said, because then he still did and that is what he thought marriage counseling might help him to show her.

"What does fucking love mean when you're always taking overtime shifts to make extra money," Darla said, and then Clayton saw the therapist give Darla the stink eye when she knew Darla wasn't looking and he knew that they were at an impasse. He could find no way to make Darla happy.

Clayton sighed, waiting for the therapist to jump in and save him.

"You love being a police officer more than our marriage," Darla said. "More than Maria."

"Not more than Maria," Clayton responded from the pureness of his hapless soul.

The therapist imperceptibly shook her head from her position between the two spouses. Darla looked both bereft and elated from her club chair on the right side of their counselor. Her eyes said "A-hah" at his admission.

Clayton knew that his goose was cooked.

Later the therapist and his own lawyer consoled him with the fact that Maria was a healthy and resilient child and that the effort that Darla was not willing to put into her marriage she was willing to put into her parenting. When Darla finally remarried she chose both a good man and a good stepfather who will always make far more money than Clayton. The second husband's money has made Darla much happier and Clayton can see this. Money can buy certain types of contentment, and people who try to pretend otherwise are deluded he thinks. Love is not enough. Both Clayton and the Beatles learned this, the hard way.

Darla's husband is not a Mormon, and this has been a point of consolation for Clayton. In the long run he knows that Darla would not have been happy as a Mormon — she likes her Starbucks, her diet Coke, and her chardonnay all far too much to live within the strictures of Mormonism. Nor would Darla have easily accepted the religion's tenet that purports that when Jesus Christ returns to the earth it will be to Missouri rather than Jerusalem. Missouri is a nice enough state, but far from hallowed ground in the eyes of any Nebraskan. Clayton also knows that he would have vigorously protested Maria joining the Church of the Latter Day Saints. His mother is a devout Roman Catholic and his brother Erik, a Lutheran minister, and neither would have been thrilled about Maria converting. Clayton would have felt it like a below the belt blow. To be made a cuckold and then to lose his wife and daughter to the other man's faith would have been too much for him.

The Mormon Church seems to be filled with very good-looking young men who are attractive to teenage girls and women. These boys ride around Omaha on bicycles with the *Book of Mormon* in their backpacks. As a police officer Clayton was glad to learn that Jacob Smith was over eighteen, because he was certain that Darla seduced the missionary. Not that his ex-wife isn't a looker, she was and is, and Jacob probably wanted to do what they were doing, but Darla was very unhappy at the time. Unhappiness clouds judgment. Everything could have been much worse if Darla had had sex with someone under the age of eighteen. For a time Clayton worried that the young man might turn on Darla, threatening her with a police report, explaining that he was just seventeen and that he felt abused by her. Intercourse between an adult and someone under the age of eighteen is a sex crime in most states. The age of seventeen is a no man's land in the area of predatory sexual practices. A Douglas County judge might have dropped the charge, but the accusation would have damned Darla in the newsprint of the *Omaha World Herald*, and in the eyes of Omahans, forever.

But Darla's Mormon missionary loved her, and she talked about him a lot during their marriage counseling sessions. Long after they stopped seeing each other Jacob would mail cards and packages to her from Star Valley, Wyoming. In his letters, Jacob continued to encourage Darla to join the Mormon Church. This never happened. Darla is still a very active member of the Evangelical Lutheran Church of America, as is Maria. Clayton's brother Erik officiated at Maria's confirmation.

Eight years into his divorce Clayton still misses his marriage, particularly on Sunday evenings. He misses singing along to songs on the radio with Maria and Darla as they drove home from visiting Darla's mom, Louise, in Fremont on Sunday afternoons. He misses the early morning weekend runs that he used to do with Darla during the warm weather months. He relished the routines of married life.

Walking the family's basset hound, Clarence, and mowing the lawn are events that Clayton loves to do over and over again in his nighttime dreams. The dreams comfort him. He feels that they are a gift to him from his unconscious, or from God.

In her voicemail message, Darla demands that Clayton be firm with Maria in regards to this misspent money, but Clayton knows that he can only be so firm with either his daughter or his former wife. Thank goodness, Maria is even more upset in her voicemail than her mother. Maria is abject in her apologies, promising complete repayment and then she says, "I have a terrible sunburn, Dad" and bursts into a flood of tears. Clayton knows that Maria has been a cakewalk compared to many other children and that even a mild firmness with her will be more than enough punishment.

Clayton's sense of loss has bled its way into early Monday morning. He tries to shake it off as he walks into the Omaha Police Department Headquarters on 15th Street. He appreciates the ritual of entering the building, the greetings from colleagues as he passes through security, and the taste of his milky coffee as he climbs the three flights of interior stairs to the fourth floor. Clayton makes his way across the floor, taking comfort in the rigid grid of cubicles and their demarcations of rank.

Cubicles remind him of beehives and honeycombs, hard work and its sweetness. As he turns the corner into his cubicle he sees The Bird sitting on the other side of his desk, looking out his window. The window is an achievement and the kind of perk that only a public servant can truly appreciate.

"Hello," he says.

"Sergeant Santos-Anderson?"

"Yes."

"I am Iris Murphy. Bob O'Malley said that he thought that you could be of assistance to me."

For a moment Clayton soaks up The Bird's language. Her extreme politeness is well known among judges, police officers, and the Douglas County Attorney's Office. She is known to be formal, pointed, and thorough during cross-examinations as a public defender. No one in Omaha speaks like The Bird, but The Bird. Courthouse wags will imitate her, "*Just how did you decide to stop Mr. Sanchez's car, Officer Hermann? The initial cause, I mean. Do you have a reading from a radar device that you could share with the court?*" ratcheting their voices up a notch, giving it a hoity-toity East Coast inflection.

The Bird's courtesy is consistent and constant in the courtroom. She never leads with humor. She never buys drinks at the legal watering holes. The moral soul can be a dangerous matter in a trial. Justice is as gray as life. Police officers have been known to embroider facts, remember differently, to fib when necessary, and certain prosecutors will often aid and abet this nature in cops. When The Bird goes to trial, she goes to win. She takes no prisoners.

"Who the hell does she think she is?" is often the bitter question put forth by Omaha's finest caught in truth stretching by Iris Murphy, as defendants have walked free, charges have been dropped, or sentences are limited to the time already served.

Cops resent Ms. Murphy, as the judges always refer to her, because they see her work, her dress, and her language as a betrayal of roots. Her old man was a decorated firefighter, a hero, and a guy's guy. Jack Murphy was known to be fearless in the face of a burning building. Retired cops say that he was "a man known for more courage than sense." Legend has it that the words "Irish, Catholic, Democrat, Proud" are carved into Jack Murphy's headstone and that this epitaph caused a great consternation among the very Catholic and very Republican-leaning administrators of the Calvary Cemetery.

As he sits down behind his desk Clayton takes the time to look at The Bird. He has glimpsed her pulling open one of the heavy doors of Saint Mary Magdalene Church to attend the 7:00 a.m. Mass on the mornings that he walks the streets of downtown Omaha to reach his goal of 10,000 steps on his pedometer. In a brisk wind, Clayton has seen her sway on high heels while the canary-colored cape that she wears in spring flutters as she makes her way into the Douglas County Courthouse. Clayton has never met The Bird in a courtroom, or anywhere else for that matter.

Every police officer in Omaha knows The Bird, as does every judge and everyone in the Douglas County Attorney's office. She is known for her brightly colored and apparently expensive clothing outside of the courtroom. Iris Murphy stands out. Clayton heard a bailiff once say that, "The Bird looks like New York." Looking like New York is okay in Omaha among the denizens of the Old Market or people who live in Dundee or Fair Acres, but it is not the way that women dress in Millard or Elkhorn or even Saint Paul. The first thing that Clayton notices about Iris Murphy is that her face is pretty, quite pretty. He knows that she must be in her early sixties, but her age is not written into her skin. She is dressed in a well-cut, lavender-colored suit. Clayton Santos-Anderson leans across his desk between its neat piles. He is drawn to the care that Iris Murphy has taken in putting herself together. All of this effort on The Bird's part before she walked into his cubicle by the window impresses him.

The Bird reminds him of his mother, Yolanda, and her sisters Rachel and Anita. Mexican-American women embrace color. They love beauty. They go out into the world showing themselves at their best. Color, like spice, in the middle-western regions of the United States is seen as sensual thus probably sinful, if not just plain foreign. To spend money on beauty is seen as wasteful and morally suspect like wearing a fur coat. In general, the women of Omaha live with Great Cuts hair, Capri pants from Target and Walmart, and the parts of outfits that they find on sale at Von Maur. They live this way on principle. Darla, however, dresses beautifully. His ex-wife is a well put-together woman, as is his daughter, and this costs money. Over the years Clayton has paid these bills with overtime pay. He likes a well-dressed woman. It is within his genetic code to appreciate The Bird.

"I have a problem, Sergeant Santos-Anderson," Iris Murphy says to him. Then she pauses before adding, "Actually two problems."

"Yes," he says, picking up a pen.

"On Saturday night, the day when the tornadoes were predicted, I was walking home from dinner with two friends," The Bird tells him. "Dark was falling. Specifically, it could be described as dusk. I could see my house from 50th Street. We were only two blocks away. The three of us heard the crash of glass. Then we ran to the house and found my storm door window shattered and a baseball in the bushes by the side of the porch."

Clayton cannot imagine any woman running in shoes like The Bird is wearing now, but it is not a point that he wants to make to her. He likes her black feathery boots. They seem Olympian and mythological and appropriate to her Courthouse moniker.

"Do you think that the baseball belonged to a neighbor's kid? That the kid might be too embarrassed to tell you?"

"That could be," she says, looking into his eyes. "But that would not explain the neatly mounded pile of dog excrement at the base of my back door. Of course, it was covered with shattered glass. It was very difficult to clean up. But there is more to this story."

"The second problem?"

"No, this is part of the first problem," she says, her hands moving in her lap.

"Oh," he says.

"On this past Wednesday, I visited a prisoner at the Nebraska State Penitentiary. His name is Leonard Howard."

"I know all about Leonard Howard," Clayton says, pushing back in his chair and for the first time, wondering if Iris Murphy really does hate cops. Hating cops is an accusation that he has heard leveled at her on occasion. But any time a trial goes against the prosecution cops will say things like that, especially about public defenders. They are seen as bleeding heart liberals. Attorneys who aren't good enough to do anything else but defend scumbags.

"My sister Bridget is profoundly deaf, as is Leonard. They both went to school at the Nebraska School for the Deaf and our families attended Masses for the Deaf together as well. Leonard was my first boyfriend. He broke up with me and broke my heart."

"I'm sorry," he says.

"It was a long time ago, Sergeant Santos-Anderson. There is nothing to be sorry about."

"About your sister, then," Clayton says this and feels stupid for saying it. He senses that he should be sorry for something because he realizes that Iris Murphy is not a cop-hater and that he did think badly of her without cause.

"My sister is a very happy and feisty deaf woman, Sergeant, but I do appreciate your concern."

"Why did you go visit him?"

This question, Clayton hopes, will get the conversation back on track to The Bird's two problems and away from the awkwardness of his apologies.

"He sent a letter asking me to visit him and he sent the forms along as well. So I filled out the forms and went through the procedures. I must admit that I am uncomfortable in prisons, but it felt like the right thing to do. And there is my curiosity."

"Did he say why he wanted to see you in the letter?"

"No."

"Why did you go?"

"I would like to tell you that I went to see him because he is a deaf man and because I am fluent in American Sign Language and I am sure that he doesn't have many visitors who can speak to him in ASL. But I visited him because I wanted to know why he broke up with me. I have never married. The remembrance of lost love can eat away at one sometimes." The Bird pauses to look out the window.

Clayton looks at her profile and wonders how he had missed this woman's beauty. How he could have walked past her as she struggled with the heavy doors of Saint Mary Magdalene Church and why he did not stop his truck to run and hold her elbow as the wind battered her about that day in front of the courthouse. Then she looks back at him and he sees a mist in her eyes. They are the blue-gray of the Irish eyes he grew up with in Saint Paul.

"To tell you the truth, Sergeant Santos-Anderson, I could never understand why Leonard did such a horrible thing to that police officer. It was hard for me to accept this because I loved Leonard so much, once upon a time."

"What did you talk about with Leonard Howard, Ms. Murphy?"

"Leonard wanted to tell me something."

"What was that?"

"That a man named Angelo Bartlett, another prisoner at the penitentiary, is angry with me. That Angelo Bartlett was going to get people to scare me, possibly harm me."

"Angelo Bartlett is a bad guy, Ms. Murphy."

Saying the man's name makes Clayton feel anxious. It makes him worry about the little girls of Omaha, the State of Nebraska, the United States, and the world. Bartlett frightens him because he is a tough, unforgiving pimp and he has done things to children that Clayton finds terrifying. Sergeant Santos-Anderson handles property crime where people are rarely hurt. It is not unusual for Clayton to see his perpetrators out on the street after short stints of incarceration. They will give him a cocky greeting and he will offer them a formal and polite "Hello." Clayton studies the work of burglars, is an interpreter of gang graffiti, can wax lyrical on the stunts of drunken teenagers, and knows the names of all the panhandlers at the exits of Omaha's Interstates who hold up handwritten cardboard signs asking drivers for money. He keeps close tabs on the petty criminals of his city. These men, and sometimes women, are a font of information and live by an elegant code of conduct that makes sense to them and once in awhile to Clayton. When other cops need to know what is happening on the street they will come to Clayton.

"Yes, Sergeant, he is."

"How did Leonard find this out?"

"Well, prisoners have their own sign language and Leonard, who is very smart, has been able to decode the various signs of other inmates. He is an actuary by training."

"I'm sure prisoners do use signs."

"Also Leonard can read lips quite well. He is far above average in this ability. But deaf people don't like hearing people to know how much they actually understand of the hearing world."

"Interesting."

"Leonard says that Angelo Bartlett thinks that I refused to defend him. But that is not how the Public Defender's Office works. Cases are assigned."

"Did you refuse to defend him?"

"No."

"Do you believe what Leonard Howard told you?"

"I believe that someone deliberately broke my window and left a pile of dog poop on my porch. I'm disturbed and I'm scared."

"Ms. Murphy, I'm sorry."

"The power of petty crimes, Sergeant Santos-Anderson, is that they are easy to commit and their perpetrators are hard to detect. As a woman living alone in my parents' house, every room grows to look like a place where something bad could happen. I have lost my sense of comfort."

"Do you have a security service?"

"Yes, my security service detects burglary and fire. But it doesn't detect petty maliciousness."

"Do you have a dog?"

"No."

"I would consider getting one."

"That's what Leonard said."

Clayton Santos-Anderson blushes and then says, "So these are your two problems."

"No, there is another problem."

"What is that?"

"On Wednesday afternoon, the same day that I visited Leonard, I found out that I have not only colon cancer, but cancer of the liver as well."

"I'm so sorry, Ms. Murphy."

"To be quite frank, the oncologist can buy me time, not decades and decades of time, but some years. Having cancer in these two organs is not a good thing, but I will continue to work as long as I can, taking leave when I have intensive chemotherapy. There will be some surgery," she pauses to gaze out the window again.

"I have a son, Miles, who works in Nairobi for the State Department and my sister Bridget and her family in Cincinnati, so I need to plan the time that I have wisely."

"But what does your health have to do with the Omaha Police Department?"

Clayton asks the question because he must. Cancer is not in his job description.

"Bob O'Malley says that you will be able to find out who broke my window and left a calling card of dog manure," The Bird looks directly in Clayton's eyes as she says this. "Bob says that you could put it together because you know almost all of the petty criminals in Omaha and that you will be able to talk to them for me."

"Lieutenant O'Malley is a fine man and I appreciate his support, but these criminals tend to be very hard to find and to prosecute," Clayton says, thinking that Bob O'Malley makes it sound like he goes to lunch with the perpetrators, takes notes, and then makes the arrests.

Bob O'Malley is a homicide lieutenant who can be a fucking pain in the ass. Bob loves drama and he has no respect for the importance of neighborhood policing and the issue of petty crimes, until he needs information from the street. Bob calls Clayton when he needs gang graffiti interpreted and then he writes up the interpretations, as though he has a freaking Master's Degree in the language of spray-painted marks on flat surfaces. Never does O'Malley mention the assistance of Sergeant Santos-Anderson, or anyone else in the non-emergency world of policing.

"It's the stress, Sergeant Santos-Anderson, and the worry. My oncologist said to avoid unnecessary stress. I don't expect you to apprehend the criminal, but somehow, if you could get the word out on the street that I am ill."

"Pardon me?"

"I would even pay them to stop."

"You're not going to pay petty criminals to stop, Ms. Murphy," he said, pushing back his desk chair.

"I'm sorry."

"This is Omaha. They'll be arrested. We're not a Third World country held hostage by the underclass and controlled by a wealthy few."

"But it's a baseball and dog excrement and the police officer who responded was not impressed when I told her about Leonard and what Leonard said. The police officer filled out the report, but I could tell that she didn't want to do it. And to tell you the truth, Bob O'Malley probably wouldn't even have taken my call but for the fact that our dads were close friends as firefighters."

Iris Murphy, The Bird, is weeping. She has covered her pretty face with the palms of her hands. Clayton, whose eyes and ears have been glued on her, now realizes that every cubicle on the fourth floor has grown silent. The sound of her sobs resonates through the silences. He reaches into his desk drawer where he keeps a box of Kleenex and pulls out three that he hands to her.

"Thank you."

"First, you know, I will need to call the prison."

The Bird nods her head.

"This may not go easy on Leonard Howard, Ms. Murphy. He could be lying. They may also want to talk to Angelo Bartlett, and Angelo Bartlett could get wind of Leonard Howard and that might put him in a very dangerous position. Bartlett is a very bad man. You will probably have to return to the prison to file a report. They may want to interview you. You should have reported this on Wednesday."

"I know. I'm sorry. I was in a kind of shock and I had to get back to Omaha for my appointment with the oncologist."

"You have nothing to be sorry about," Clayton says. "I will explain the situation to the Visitation Coordinator at the penitentiary."

Clayton can feel the crap raining down upon him. The hours he will have to put into this case that will turn out to be a teenager's prank. Leonard Howard is a dick and a mean angry drunk, and he is probably just lying because addicts lie like they piss — everyday and multiple times. But if Clayton finds the perpetrator and if there is any connection to Angelo Bartlett and if Leonard Howard is telling the truth, then Bob O'Malley, dickhead that he is, will swoop up the press, taking credit for solving the case because he made the referral to the unnamed sergeant in Property Crime. This is just the reality of Monday mornings.

"Sergeant Santos-Anderson, I asked Leonard why he broke up with me and he said that he doesn't like the way that I dress." The Bird says this in a quiet voice. Her eyes set on some distant point on the other side of Clayton's window. "Leonard said he thinks that I'm stuck up, or something to that effect."

"Ms. Murphy, he's a felon."

The Bird turns her eyes back on him.

"Sergeant Santos-Anderson, there are many felons who think the world of me, but I thought that you might need to know what this particular felon thinks of me. Leonard doesn't really like me, but my small hope is that he does not want me harmed. I don't want Leonard harmed in prison, but that in so many ways is out of my hands. All of this information, oddly personal as it is, may turn out to be pertinent somehow to your research. Or not, and if it is not, I apologize for bending your ear about it."

Clayton's heart expands. The beautiful Bird sings for him. She has built a bridge of admission in that she has revealed the fact that she once loved a bad man. The crimes of women are uniquely tied to money and bad men, low self-esteem and foolishness. The sergeant feels himself falling in love with the public defender.

He clears his throat.

"Be that as it may. Leonard Howard is a fool, a felon, and he has bad eyesight. These are facts. But getting on with the task at hand, I have some questions that I must ask you and some forms that we will need to fill out." Sergeant Clayton Santos-Anderson powers up his computer and puts in his password.

The Bird smiles as Clayton hears the clicking sounds of computer keyboards all over the fourth floor of the Omaha Police Department. Phones ring and bodies move between cubicles. His day has begun in the world of Property Crime.

The Enigma of Iris Murphy

PAUL SIMMONS SEES MARTHA BERGER sitting with Iris Murphy at
a table by the window on the second floor of Mark's Bistro, a restaurant
that is a few blocks from each of their homes in the Dundee neighborhood of Omaha. They are drinking iced tea. The two women never have
a glass of wine when they eat dinner with him. They understand that he
comes to their monthly meals from his Saturday afternoon Alcoholics
Anonymous meetings, and Martha and Iris know that it will always be
hard for Paul to watch anyone else drink. Paul loved his cocktails —
their complicated mixture, scents, and seasonal colors. He still dreams
of them. Not all of Paul's friends and family are so gracious about this
issue. Martha and Iris know that he always goes to AA meetings on
Saturday afternoons because he must. The support of the meeting helps
him get through Saturday evening without a drink. Eighteen years into
sobriety and Paul still misses alcohol and the social lubrication it once
gave his system. It is not easy being a sixty-three-year-old gay man in
Omaha, Nebraska, but he has stuck it out through a nasty divorce and
many years of being sober. Since being shoved out of the closet by his
former wife, Cissy, Paul has had a series of lovers, but never a partner,
and when other friends dropped him from their society after his outing,
Iris and Martha stood steady by his side.

The women look up and wave to him, and he basks in the glow of
their affection as he makes his way across the small room. He leans in

to kiss Martha and then Iris. Martha smells of White Linen and Iris of Cool Water. He can remember when they dabbed sandalwood and musk at their pulse points, the overpowering scents of youth.

"Darlings, you look beautiful," he tells them.

Paul's words are true. Iris and Martha have each grown even more attractive in the years past middle age, whatever middle age is. He has long thought that it is sad that these two women, best friends since their fourteenth year on earth, did not fall in love with each other way back when. If they had, then life would have been much simpler for the two of them. But life is rarely simple in Paul's estimation.

"Let's order, and then I want to hear all the news that is not about tornadoes," he says as he pulls out his chair. "I'm sorry about Creston and Norfolk and Kansas and Oklahoma. Or climate change, I'm sorry about that as well, but enough about the weather already."

Paul orders a glass of lemonade and then looks at the menu. He loves caffeine, but he can't drink it on Saturday night. The least little bit of caffeine past noon on Saturday will keep him sleepless until the wee hours of Sunday morning. Breaking with his custom of ordering soup and salad, Paul asks the server for the macaroni and cheese, a house specialty.

"Paul, you never order pasta," Martha says.

Paul smiles.

"It will give my Lipitor something to do for a change."

"I love macaroni and cheese. It made Friday dinners palatable for me as a child," Iris says. "I hated it when Mom served fish sticks or tuna casserole."

"But you always order the warm spinach salad," Paul says. "Why don't you order the macaroni and cheese if you love it so much?"

"Sometimes I think that what I like best is the memory of its flavor and texture and that I'll be disappointed if I eat it now. I'm afraid it won't taste as I remember it. And since I'm nearing my dotage, I want certain things to stay unchanged," Iris says.

"Speak for yourself on the topic of dotage," Paul says, irritated with Iris's habit of referring to her age, their age, as if death was around the corner for her. Iris has always looked younger than her age, while he never has. Paul knows that he holds Iris's youthful appearance against her and that this feeling is a petty trait in his character.

"Nothing is as unblemished as a childhood memory," Martha says with equanimity.

Desperate to keep Iris off of what Paul considers to be melancholy topics, including tornadoes, he leads them into a round of Omaha gossip and political factoids as they eat their dinners, waiting until dessert to divulge the big events of their lives. He notices that Iris is quiet, letting Martha tell a story about a local politician who is heavily invested in companies selling supplies to the military without comment. Paul talks about Bob Kerrey returning to Nebraska to run for the United States Senate, but Iris says nothing, not even about Bob Kerrey whom she adores. Martha looks across the table at Iris whose focus is on her salad and then at Paul with a raise of her eyebrows. He shrugs his shoulders in response to Martha, signaling that he is uncertain as to what is behind Iris's reticence. Paul decides to play offense and tell his news first this evening. If dour news is coming from Iris about some indigent client of hers or that Miles has broken his leg, or his heart, then Paul wants to bask in the joy of his good fortune first. Over the years he has found Iris a bit dramatic when describing her work at the public defender's office. It is the Irish in Iris that tends to make her a good girl martyr. Even thinking this bitchy thought makes Paul prickle with guilt, but he pushes it away, thinking "Well, it's true, God damn it. Everyone knows that Iris Bernadette Murphy is a saint." He feels disloyal and honest simultaneously as he often does when pondering the enigma of Iris.

The server appears, and the women order the crème brulee while Paul asks for the chocolate mousse. They drink cappuccinos while he nurses a pot of herbal tea.

Martha begins by looking at each of them and saying, "I want to hear news of you and yours."

Before Iris can speak, Paul looks around the room and then leans into the table to whisper, "I'm in love and it's real."

Martha looks at Iris and Iris looks at Martha then both of them turn their eyes on Paul.

Iris says, "Congratulations."

"Who is he?" Martha asks.

"His name is David Richmond. I met him at an investment program on the distribution of assets. I'm wild about him and more importantly he's crazy about me."

"But we saw you in March, Paul. Four weeks ago. How long have you known him?" Iris looks neutral as she asks him this. It is a court-room look that Paul has seen her use many times in and out of court.

"As I said, I met him at a meeting that my investment club attended, and that was in October. A few weeks later I saw him again at the Oma-ha Playhouse and I took a moment to say hello and David asked me out for coffee after the play. We've been meeting weekly since then, and I didn't want to say anything because I wasn't certain where it was going until recently."

Paul realizes that he is speaking in hushed tones, afraid that the cus-tomers at the other tables will hear and judge him. He will always feel embarrassed about being gay, and he is embarrassed about being em-barrassed, but he cannot change that about himself. What other people think of him, he knows, matters too much to him, but he never has this worry with Martha and Iris. There is very little they don't know about his private life. Between them there are stories that only Iris knows and there are details that only Martha is aware of. Each woman has been sworn to secrecy not to tell the other and it is apparent to Paul that neither has.

"Tell us about him, Paul," Martha says.

"David is from California and he's seventy. He has children in the area and he moved to Omaha to watch his grandchildren grow up. His partner died in San Diego eight years ago. He's a Unitarian and he's heavily invested in Berkshire Hathaway."

"David Richmond's rich," Martha says. "And older than you are."

"He looks younger," Paul says, not meaning to say it, but it's true. David is gorgeous for seventy.

"Paul, you're in love," Iris says. "I'm so happy for you."

He can see tears in Iris's eyes and happiness and once again he feels guilty. Life would have been far easier for him if he had married and divorced Iris Murphy rather than Cissy Fremont Simmons. A divorce from Iris would have landed them a glowing article in the *Advocate* about amicable partings for the middle-aged married man coming out of the closet. Cissy has compared her marriage to Paul Simmons in terms of the Holocaust, a comparison that is cruelly inaccurate and tasteless. But Cissy is rich and used to saying whatever she wants to say with impunity. The reason Paul didn't marry Iris was because he was in love with idea of Cissy and her money. Money attracts money, as his dad always said. But Cissy also pursued him and performed sexual acts on him and for him that were like none he could have imagined. Mornings after their rapacious escapades Paul was convinced that at the worst he was only bisexual. His sexual attraction for Cissy waned within the first twenty-four months of their union. New is only new once. But by that time Cissy was pregnant and Paul was fumbling his way through a very exciting affair with Cissy's hairdresser Louis. The product of marital procreation brought his son Max into the world and then his daughter Molly. Sex with Louis sustained him as did drink and lots of it while his children were in preschool and elementary school, but then, of course, Cissy hired a detective. His friendships with Iris and Martha were the ballast that supported him through the divorce and rehab a few years after that. The process of both was long and ugly.

The Enigma of Iris Murphy 39

"When do we get to meet him?" Martha asks.

"Can he come to next month's dinner?" Paul asks, certain that Iris will veto the idea.

"That's breaking our hard and fast and only rule," Martha says, looking at Iris.

"It's time we break that rule," Iris tells them.

"*Why?*" Paul and Martha ask in unison.

"Well, say I get called away, the two you will always have David to hold up my end of the conversation."

"You invented this group," Martha says. "You're our high priestess. You've never allowed us to miss a monthly meal together in twenty-eight years."

"She's right, Iris. That's never going to happen. We have to live by our one and only rule — that the meal is about the three of us and no one else is invited. I was stupid to bring it up. We'll just take David out for Sunday brunch."

Breaking rules is very unlike Iris and this disturbs Paul. Iris is boringly honest and everlastingly earnest, a true Pollyanna. Even when she gave birth to Miles out-of-wedlock, as they used to say, and gave Omaha's chattering classes something to mull over for months, she was painstakingly up front about the whole gestation to the great embarrassment of her dad. Firefighters' daughters were always to be vestal virgins despite the randy nature of men like Jack Murphy.

"Martha, do you have news?" Iris asks, effectively changing the subject.

"I finished the Grantham project for the bank and I'm going to Greece with Laura in October. That's my news. Oh, and I'm buying a bicycle by cashing in some of my many unused sick days. I'm going to attach a wicker basket to its handlebars and ride around Dundee on my days off. Pooh Dog can ride in the basket."

Paul smiles. The image of Martha in a French fisherman's sweater pedaling around Dundee on her bicycle makes his day. This is the kind of news he enjoys. Everyone will notice Martha and Pooh Dog, her Cairn terrier. They will mention it to Paul and Paul will say, "Oh, that's my friend, Martha Berger, on her bike. She's a vice-president at First National Bank. Her dad was Ed Berger, an executive at Conagra."

There is a pause in the conversation. Each person takes a bite of dessert. Paul dreads the idea of what Iris may offer as news. She has been throwing around the idea of volunteering for an NGO in Iraq or Afghanistan. Iris has weeks and weeks of vacation time she has never used. So instead of taking a vacation she wants to go and help women in Baghdad, or the court system in Afghanistan. Iris has been completely against the war in Iraq and she has never talked about George W. Bush at their dinners out of respect for Paul's Republican upbringing, but she did allow the Omaha Democratic Party to put up a giant John Kerry sign in her front yard in 2004 and an Obama sign in 2008. People wrote letters to the editor of the *Omaha World Herald* about both signs. Her decision to do so was either heroic or scandalous, depending on who was writing the letter. Goodness knows what Iris will do this election season. She adores and loves Barack Obama.

Possibly Iris is going to work on another legal project for one of the Indian tribes on the reservations in Thurston County. Paul will have to listen, once again, to the trials and tribulations of what has been done to America's indigenous peoples. Iris is not starry-eyed about the problems of any of the people she serves. Nor does she ever insinuate that other people should be doing what she is doing, but Paul feels guilty when Iris is away helping the needy and he is lying supine on a chaise lounge beside the pool at Happy Hollow Country Club. Paul braces himself for some sort of Mother Theresa announcement, but Iris doesn't speak.

Finally the silence at the table extends beyond polite into awkward and he blurts out,

"So, Iris, what's your news this evening?"

Iris looks at Paul and then at Martha.

"I did mention in February or March that I was going to have a colonoscopy?"

"No, I don't remember you mentioning that," Martha says.

"A colonoscopy is not news, Iris, that's healthcare," Paul says, trying to relieve his voice of the irritation that he is beginning to feel. "News is like you're going to Chicago and you have a reservation at Charlie Trotter's. Or Miles is getting married. That's news."

"Now, Paul," Martha says, raising her right hand off of the table. "Let Iris speak."

"Well in late February I had a colonoscopy," Iris tells them, looking out the window, her hands beginning to move nervously in her lap. "The gastroenterologist found something. It was biopsied, and I have cancer of the colon."

"I know so many people who have had that surgery and then boom they do the chemo and they're back on the tennis court in six weeks," Paul says, because he wants to say something that sounds positive, something less bitchy than "a colonoscopy is not news." Cancer is news, and Paul knows this. But now he can't quite remember any one person who has been diagnosed with colon cancer and then had the surgery and chemo and was back on the tennis courts in six weeks, but there must be someone in Omaha who fits this description. Paul knows he probably heard some form of this story at an AA meeting, because he hears everything at AA.

Iris takes Paul's hand and squeezes it gently as she continues to look out the window. Her hand is shaking. She returns it to her own lap.

"Before deciding on a plan for surgery and oncology for my colon cancer, the surgeon and the oncologist wanted CT scans of the area around my colon and the nearby organs. I worked the scan in around a court date, and to tell you the truth I didn't do it as quickly as the doctors wanted. But cutting to the chase of the story, this week the oncologist told me what the radiologist found."

Iris stops. Her hands are moving as she continues to look out the window. Paul knows that she is signing. It is a nervous habit of hers. He thinks that she says more in signs than she will speak aloud in words. It is a habit that he finds irritating most of the time, but it is Iris's second language. Her sister Bridget is deaf.

"Iris, what did the doctor find?" Martha asks.

Iris blinks. A tear slides down the side of her face as her hands move into the space in front of her body, saying something that neither he nor Martha can interpret. Paul remembers the first time he saw Iris. It was at the University of Nebraska College of Law. She was sitting in the front row of a lecture hall. The seats on either side of her were empty. With her hair pulled back in a ponytail, Iris looked like a child, hardly more than a young teenager. It bothered him that she was alone. Even then Paul's instinct was to protect her. So he walked down the steps and sat beside her though he hated sitting in the front rows of lecture halls. Iris looked like a sparrow among hawks, as the boys filed in to sit around the two of them.

"I have cancer of the liver as well," Iris says.

"My God, Iris," Martha says, her composure shaken.

"Are they certain? Doctors do make mistakes, you know, no matter how much they scream about the need for tort reform. There's a place for tort law in this world," Paul says in a raised voice. People at other tables turn their heads to look at him.

Paul hates doctors. He hates the smugness of all their smartness. He resents the way physicians seem to crowd the stage at dinner parties. He can't stand the fact that they peer into the recesses and cavities of his body and he cannot do the same. And when Cissy remarried she remarried a cardiologist while Paul was in rehab. The cardiologist owns a place in Aspen and he was Ak-Sar-Ben's fucking King of Quivera.

Somehow Cissy got their wedding photograph into *Town & Country*. It was awful. Paul despises doctors. And now a goddamned fucking doctor has given Iris, his bedrock best friend, a diagnosis of colon and liver cancer. May that fool roast in hell someday.

"Setting aside the issues of tort reform for a minute, yes, I do think that the doctors are correct in their diagnosis," Iris says, leaning forward with a grimace.

"How do you feel?" Martha asks, giving him a glare that says "Shut up."

"At work, I feel good. I'm busy. I'm needed. But at home I feel some discomfort. The pain sent me to my internist in the first place."

"What do the doctors want to do?" Paul asks, thinking that this is the right question and Martha will approve of it. He is beginning to feel a sense of panic.

Losing Iris is not something he has ever considered. He loves Iris. If he hadn't been so stupidly besotted with Cissy and with the idea that he was going to wake up straight like the rest of the world he would have married Iris and been step-father to Miles and then divorced Iris in a much nicer fashion than his divorce from Cissy. Possibly he would have imbibed less, possibly. Of course, there would be no Max and Molly if he had married Iris, and that is the whole problem with revisionist histories, he thinks. Fuck it all.

"Would the two of you mind walking me home?" Iris asks, signaling to the server to bring them their bills.

At this moment, Paul Simmons would love to have a drink, many drinks, as a matter of fact. But he has promised himself that he will never have a drink again until he is dying, really and truly dying. Then he will drink Manhattans and gin and tonics and dirty martinis and single malt scotch and all the new-fangled beers that they are serving all over Omaha in the bars that he never enters. In Paul's vision of his death, Iris and Martha are serving him the drinks as they wipe his fevered brow.

The drinks taste wonderful mixed with the morphine dripping into a port in his vein and he feels safe because Iris and Martha are with him.

For many years on the three Saturdays of every month when Paul did not eat dinner with Iris and Martha after his twelve-step meeting and before he met David Richmond, Paul would console himself with this imagined drunken death scene. Since meeting David and promising David that he would be faithful to both him and to AA, Paul has not spent Saturday nights alone. For the very first time in his life, Paul has begun to feel like what he believes happy heterosexuals feel, safe, comfortable, breathing in and out, sleeping without fear.

The server appears and Paul takes all three checks from him.

"I'm paying."

"Paul, that's against the rules," Iris says.

"Tonight, the rules have changed," he says, as he hands over his Visa card.

Neither woman disagrees.

The Dog

D<small>R</small>. E<small>ZRA</small> H<small>OLLOWAY</small> <small>PULLS UP TO HIS HOUSE</small> on St. Charles Place. St. Charles Place is a cul-de-sac cut into a hill off of Erie Avenue; it is not far from Hyde Park Square in Cincinnati. From the driver's seat of his white Aerostar Van, Ezra can see his wife, Anna, pushing the baby stroller back and forth on the sidewalk in front of their home.

It is mid-April in 2010. A few trees are still blooming, but most have dropped their petals and now stand fully leafed. Baseball season has begun. Christ has risen on Easter Sunday while Moses has again led his people out of Egypt during the days of Passover. Life is mild, and the out-of-doors calls out to the living to abandon their indoor chores for the day. Plants and animals awaken, survive, and have begun to multiply. There is death and dying as well, but it is squashed by spring full-bore. Ezra knows that April is rarely the cruelest month of all. He reserves that caption for cold, drear February when far too many hearts are broken on Saint Valentine's Day and hopes for copulation and possible procreation are dashed by metaphorical frostbite.

On the front porch of the Holloways' slate blue two-story home sits a dog. The dog is a mixed breed. He has the head of a retriever, the coloration of a German shepherd, and what appears to be the thick fur of a chow. Ezra senses both the dog's hunger and fear, and that the animal has been waiting for him to arrive. Anna pushes the baby stroller around the van to the driver's door, as he rolls down the window.

"Sweetie," she says. "Could you take care of the dog? I want to nurse Charlie before we eat dinner."

Charlie whimpers, accenting his mother's point.

"Sure," Ezra says, opening his door as Anna pushes the stroller back to the sidewalk beside the lawn.

As he steps out of the van, Ezra looks up into the gaze of Horace Mann, a marmalade-colored Maine coon cat who is sitting on the window seat of the landing between the two floors of the house. From his perch the majestic Horace Mann peers down upon his humans and Ezra feels the scowl emanating from Horace's heart. Horace, he knows, must be aware of the dog on his front porch. It means that the house will have company until Ezra can find the animal a situation. This kind of scenario never pleases Horace Mann, but it is something he is willing to endure for short periods of time.

Animals have appeared unexpectedly in Ezra Holloway's life long before he went to veterinary school at Ohio State University. The first was a dog brought to him by his maternal grandparents, quite unannounced. She was a liver spotted Dalmatian with blue eyes, whose exact age was unknown. His grandfather, Jack Murphy, drove the dog to Cincinnati from Nebraska. She had been abandoned at the Omaha firehouse where Grandpa Jack worked. Grandpa Jack did not tell Ezra's mother about the impending gift of a dog. Bridget Murphy-Holloway blew her stack in both sign language and verbal tics and exhalations that sounded both angry and obscene when Grandpa Jack and Nana Honora walked into the house with a Dalmatian on a leash. The angrier Ezra's mother became in her communications, the more his grandfather grinned.

While his mom raged at his grandfather the Dalmatian wandered into the kitchen where she found eight-year-old Ezra who was mixing together a batch of home made soap bubbles. The dog bumped Ezra's hip, rubbing his face against his ribcage. Ezra set aside his concoction to pick up the leash that was attached to the tail-wagging dog, walking her through the dining room and into the front room around the small scrum of adults who were standing near his dad's Baldwin baby grand piano.

His mother's hands knew no fury like the fury they expressed when her father thwarted her.

"A boy ought to have a dog," Jack Murphy signed to his daughter as his wife Honora stood behind him. "Miles has a dog and he's six and Ezra's eight and it's only fair."

Ezra's dad, Walter, stood next to Honora, where he signed, "It will be okay, Bridget," to his wife.

"Look," Jack Murphy signed to his daughter, "Ezra wants the dog."

Everyone in the room knew that his irascible grandfather signed the truth. Ezra did want the dog, and his mom and dad knew that he wanted the dog. By bringing the dog, his Grandpa Jack had decided to take the matter into his own hands, believing that all boys needed dogs. (This is something that Ezra agrees with in spirit, but as a veterinarian he knows that all children need responsible parents who will care for both them and the pets of a household with humanity. It is Ezra's opinion that a child should never be the responsible party for pets or other children.)

"That's not the point, Dad. Don't you think Walter and I deserve some warning about a dog?" his mother signed. "Some choice?"

What Ezra remembers is that the Dalmatian felt like home to him from the moment that she nuzzled him in the kitchen. Between the dog and the boy there was an immediate communication; Ezra felt chosen. In his mind he could picture the dog's need to squat, the stream of golden urine, and sense the relief that would come to the animal from this act. It has always been this way with Ezra and animals. While his mother's hands continued to fly, Ezra pushed the loop of the dog's leash halfway up his arm, so that he could sign to his family,

"The dog needs to pee," but none of the adults paid attention to him.

Then he said, "The dog needs to pee," and his father and grandmother turned to watch him lead the Dalmatian onto the screened in porch and from there, out the door to the front yard, as the argument in sign language continued.

As Ezra walked the bounding dog up and down Pandora Avenue he came to realize that she was a bitch and that her name was Daisy. The image of a singular daisy in a field of blue grass rolled into his thoughts like electricity connecting to a light bulb. When their neighbor Hiram Lauterwasser's Grand Prix backfired, as it always did, Daisy kept walking, ignoring the noise. When Tommy Ryan drove past them in his Celica with the thumping beat of LL Cool J's *Going Back to Cali* blaring out of the car's open windows, Daisy took no notice. Of course, she barked up a storm when she saw Mrs. Kelso's cat, Henrietta, sunning herself on the Kelsos' cement steps next to a planter filled with scarlet geraniums. Daisy dragged Ezra halfway into the street in pursuit of a squirrel that she had sighted in her peripheral vision. Mrs. Cantwell was driving very slowly down the road in her little red Honda Civic as he pulled Daisy out of the street and onto the safety of the sidewalk.

Mrs. Cantwell bellowed at him, "Ezra Holloway, you stay out of the street and take that dog home right now, or I'll be calling your daddy." Then she looked at Daisy and said, "Dalmatians are the bravest dogs in a fire that there are."

Thelma Cantwell was an African American woman who spent her senior years on Pandora Avenue, acting as a free security service for the neighborhood and spying on Ezra Holloway's every move, or so he thought. She took an extra interest in him, Ezra knew, because his dad, Walter, was black and his mom, Bridget, was white and deaf. In retrospect it seemed to Ezra that Mrs. Cantwell felt that she had to groom him in the proper ways of being black, because black women often held the white wives of black men in low regard. The sentiments of these women were that white women did not know about proper skin and hair care for children of color, nor were they the best type of Christians. In Mrs. Cantwell's opinion the best type of Christians were always members of an African Methodist Episcopal congregation. Roman Catholics,

The Dog

like his mother, were not exactly Christian enough in her estimation.

Ezra mother's deafness also perplexed Mrs. Cantwell. She seemed unnerved when Bridget answered the door and offered her a pad of paper so that they could communicate. When Ezra or his dad would come into the front room to interpret for Bridget, Mrs. Cantwell would raise her voice as though it might help Bridget to understand the interpreted words. Walter Holloway thoroughly enjoyed Mrs. Cantwell's raised voice. Even as a small child, Ezra felt appalled by Mrs. Cantwell. But his dad held to the point-of-view that "Mrs. Cantwell is a character and life would be boring without characters," and his mother agreed.

"When you are old like us you will tell your friends stories about Mrs. Cantwell," she would sign to him, laughing.

In his teenage years, when Mrs. Cantwell's raised voice turned into outright yelling, Ezra signed to his dad in exasperation,

"What's wrong with this woman?"

Walter Holloway signed back, "Son, she's lost her hearing."

Bridget Murphy-Holloway was not one to worry about what other people thought of her, particularly hearing people, including Mrs. Cantwell. Also Ezra's mom appreciated Thelma Cantwell's tattle-telling ways, as did most of the other parents on Pandora Avenue. When Mrs. Cantwell moved into a senior residence Bridget and Walter visited her at least once a month until her death.

"Blue-eyed Dalmatians are often deaf," Mrs. Cantwell told Ezra, before returning to her drive down Pandora Avenue to whatever errand that she had to run that Saturday afternoon.

Standing there on the sidewalk, watching the tail end of the red Honda move slowly down the street, Ezra knew that Mrs. Cantwell spoke the truth. What Ezra could see was an image of barking dogs and no sound. When they returned to the Holloways' yard, Daisy peed and then pooped underneath his mother's redbud tree. (The poop was something Ezra knew that he would have to learn to clean up, if he wanted to keep Daisy, which he did, but at that age he hated the number twos of any species. So he thought that he would ask his dad whose job poop clean up would be, but he knew to ask this question later.)

When Ezra took Daisy into the house he walked her past his grandparents who were sitting on the couch and listening to his father play a section of George Gershwin's *Rhapsody in Blue* on the Baldwin baby grand and into the kitchen where his mother was preparing supper and signed this to her,

"The dog's name is Daisy, and Mrs. Cantwell says she's deaf."

Bridget Murphy-Holloway believed Ezra when he told her what Mrs. Cantwell said about Daisy. Then his mom offered the dog some cooked hamburger and she began to sign to Daisy, welcoming her into their home and apologizing for the argument, explaining in unnecessary detail, Ezra thought, even at the age of eight years, that she and her dad tended to argue, but that they loved each other very much, as she would love Daisy. Daisy paid attention to his mother's hands and all of the information that they were imparting, but she paid even more attention to the hamburger.

Later the Red Bank Veterinary Clinic confirmed Daisy's deafness and explained that some breeders felt strongly about euthanizing deaf dogs, but that the Dalmatian seemed healthy and relatively adjusted for an abandoned animal. Ezra's mother was appalled when her husband signed this information to her. Her hands began to fly in indignation and she made sure that Walter translated everything that she had to say on the topic of euthanizing deaf dogs, including, "Thank goodness that God is not a dog breeder," and this final statement made the veterinarian laugh.

Daisy lived nine years with Ezra's family on Pandora Avenue. They quickly learned that she needed to be walked at least three times a day and that the walks needed to be long, if the Murphy-Holloway family wanted peace in their household. Several clients allowed Walter to bring

Daisy with him when he tuned their pianos, as did certain institutions that needed many pianos tuned on a seasonal basis. Daisy was happiest when she was riding shotgun with Walter in his van. It was in Walter's van that Daisy seemed most like the carriage dog that her ancestors had been bred to be.

The down turn in Daisy's life came on a day when Walter Holloway had been scheduled to tune two Steinway baby grand pianos at the home of Gratia Zimmerman on Observatory Avenue. Mrs. Zimmerman was both a piano instructor and a dog lover. She always invited Daisy to her house when Walter was working on the pianos. Mrs. Zimmerman was waiting for the piano tuner and his dog on her front steps when Walter pulled up on her driveway. As Walter was helping Daisy out of the van and Mrs. Zimmerman was walking towards them, a dog named Serena tore across her owner's lawn and into Mrs. Zimmerman's yard, attacking Daisy. Serena, a Briard, was new to Observatory Avenue and was allowed by her owner to be off her leash as her owner worked in the garden beds. The Briard jumped on Daisy with little or no warning, at least none that Walter or Mrs. Zimmerman could remember. Later, Walter admitted to Bridget that he was focusing that morning on what he remembered the tones of the two Steinways to be. In his mind, he was already playing the pianos when Serena lunged at Daisy. If the Briard barked a warning, as Serena's owner claimed, then like Daisy, Walter did not hear it. As the teeth of the Briard tore into her backside Daisy screamed in pain and surprise, turning on the other dog. A dogfight ensued as Serena's owner ran across the yards, screaming,

"Stop, Serena, drop the dog," but Serena ignored her.

Mrs. Zimmerman ran to turn on her hose, spraying the dogs with the water until they separated, allowing Serena's owner to grab the Briard by the collar and drag her away. Daisy was badly bitten and Walter had to abandon tuning Mrs. Zimmerman's pianos to take the dog to the Red Bank Veterinary Clinic. Many stitches and hours later, Daisy was released from the clinic with an Elizabethan plastic collar around her head and a bag full of antibiotics and ointments that had to be given and applied at specific times. Walter returned that evening to Observatory Avenue to tune the pianos and Ezra went with him while Bridget stayed at home to care for Daisy. Somehow Ezra wanted to understand the Briard and why she would attack Daisy without provocation.

While Walter tuned the pianos Ezra walked down the sidewalk to the house his father had pointed out to him as they pulled up to Mrs. Zimmerman's. The house was dark. Standing there in the dusk, Ezra was overcome with the agitated unhappiness of Serena, who he sensed was inside the home without the companionship of a human. Ezra felt the frightened irritation of a dog whose life was out of control. Images of a woman came into Ezra's mind. The woman, he understood, often left the dog alone. The man whom Serena loved the most had abandoned the woman and Serena as well. The Briard's pack had been torn asunder and the alpha member was no longer there to lead. Ezra deduced that the angry Serena attacked the deaf Daisy in her need to dominate some part of her world. Even then, as a high school junior, Ezra realized that both the dog and the woman were emotionally fragile, scarred by abandonment. These are emotions he has felt over and over again among animals and often the people who accompany them to the clinic where he works. Companion animals, especially dogs, need work to do and they need strong leadership from their humans. The Briard, Ezra knew, was in a very bad way as was his owner, and there was nothing he could do about it. Serena's owner was speaking to Walter Holloway through her lawyer and her insurance company.

Years later in veterinary school Ezra would learn what an ancient, proud, and distinguished breed the Briard is, but that night he learned how helpless a human being can feel, knowing that without changes in Serena's life that the dog's unhappiness would continue. He sensed that Serena would attack other dogs. Moreover, he understood that without a great intervention that Serena might well grow mad. Like all young veterinarians Ezra had to learn to focus on the animals he could help, or like Serena, he too might go mad.

Daisy did not heal quickly from her wounds. Her deafness became more pronounced in that she grew extraordinarily wary of anyone approaching her from the rear. Her fear of attack led to snapping and frantic barking if she was taken unawares. The trust that Daisy once had for the other dogs in the Pleasant Ridge neighborhood that surrounds Pandora Avenue was never regained. Walter, Bridget, and Ezra learned to cross the street if they saw another dog approaching. Daisy began to fail in the year after the attack, developing kidney stones and aggravated skin issues. One morning when Walter went to get Daisy for her first walk of the day he found her dead in the dog bed where she slept beneath the Baldwin baby grand. Ezra was bereft. Daisy was his first death. For weeks he was inconsolable.

Several months after Daisy's death, Bridget found a calico kitten asleep in the flower box on the steps leading up to their back door. Holding the kitten, Ezra realized that she had no name and little memory of a life before the flower box. Walter named her Petunia. No one responded to the flier describing Petunia that Bridget posted at the Pleasant Ridge Community Center. Throughout his undergraduate years at the University of Cincinnati, Petunia slept with Ezra. After he moved to Columbus for veterinary school, Petunia began to sleep with Walter and Bridget. Petunia was sweet and loving, and Ezra understood, very thankful to be found. The cat asked very little of the Murphy-Holloways and consoled them in ways that they did not know that they needed to be consoled after Daisy's death. She brought ease and affection into their home. An elderly Petunia still lives with Walter and Bridget on Pandora Avenue. Ezra adores sweet Petunia, but he knows that Horace Mann despises her.

Ezra thinks about baby Charlie as he approaches the dog that waits for him on the porch. Someday he wants Charlie to have the companionship of a dog. But it will have to be after Horace Mann passes. Horace Mann has been Ezra's friend and companion animal since graduate school days. Horace was purchased by a Dublin, Ohio woman who found him in a cage at a flea market in West Memphis, Arkansas. The woman drove the cat home and to the Ohio State University College of Veterinary Medicine.

"I had to buy him," the woman told the veterinarian examining the mangy, undernourished kitten. "He was dying in that heat and the woman selling him was a nut case. But I don't know what I'll do with him. I have two Maine coon cats already."

"I'll take him," Ezra said, from his center position in the cluster of veterinary students, observing their professor. He could feel the kitten's fear and he could envision the shadowy bodies of larger and unwelcoming Maine coon cats at the woman's house.

The professor's gaze turned towards Ezra, whose response to the woman was a breach of etiquette in the clinic. His peers at Ohio State thought of Ezra as softhearted, the kind of personality who would eventually give out far too much credit to the owners of the animals he cared for. His classmates gave him the nickname "James Herriot," after the Scottish veterinarian beloved by elderly women who watch reruns of *All Creatures Great and Small* on public television.

"Yes, but will you pay for him?"

"Whoa, now," said the examining veterinarian.

"Yes," Ezra said.

"Will you pay for this vet bill as well? I shouldn't have to pay for it if you're going to own the cat. Ohio State always overcharges."

One of his classmates snickered.

Ezra could feel Horace Mann's tension and how much the cat did not want to be with this woman and the felines in her home.

"Yes."

Everyone in the clinic assumed that Ezra adopted the unkempt kitten because of his softhearted nature. Many predicted that he would leave Columbus, Ohio with a menagerie of abandoned animals in his care, or that he would become an eccentric rural doctor and a savior to animals dropped off by the sides of country roads. None of this came to pass.

Ezra nursed the marmalade-colored kitten to abundant health, but Horace Mann — the cat's name came to Ezra in a dream — would tolerate only humans as his companions. His birth in a cattery and his short time in the lovely suburb of Dublin, Ohio, introduced him to the nasty pecking orders of cats. In their first months together, Ezra came to understand all this about Horace. The cat loved Ezra, but he was completely resistant to the idea of other animals living in their quarters. From behind the grill in his cat carrier, Horace greeted sweet Petunia with hisses whenever he and Ezra were visitors on Pandora Avenue.

What Ezra's classmates did not know that day in clinic was that Ezra's college girlfriend had called him early that morning from Cincinnati to tell him that she wanted to end their relationship and he stood among them in a stupor of grief. The ragged-looking kitten with its giant paws called out to the heartbroken young man to be loved. Inside of Ezra was a well of affection that needed to go somewhere before it turned bitter, and in front of him was a creature on an examining table that needed his protection. Responsible veterinarians and animal humane societies caution people to avoid getting a pet on impulse. The very presence of Horace in his life has caused Ezra to be far less judgmental of the pet owners he serves. For as much as he wanted to love the little Maine coon, Ezra needed even more for the kitten to love him and Horace always has.

From the beginning the bedraggled kitten could intuit that his world with Ezra would not be complete until his human had found a female, but survival without harassment was foremost in Horace Mann's mind that afternoon, not love. Horace never hisses at Anna and he allows her to pet him; he only observes baby Charlie from a safe distance. The regal cat may appear to disdain the refugees that find their way into the sanctuary room in the basement of the Holloways' home, but Ezra knows that Horace Mann is not without sympathy for their plight.

So with a quiet confidence Ezra approaches the dog on his porch. He senses that the dog knows that he is now safe. Animals realize that if they can that make their way to Ezra Holloway they will receive care and food. Somehow they know that this quiet veterinarian who speaks to them in sounds and hand gestures will find a situation for them. Whether dog or cat or parrot or laboratory rat, they intuit that Ezra will do them no harm, and this is no small thing. The dog before him, Ezra realizes, is looking for work like most dogs are. The need for industry is what humans seem to comprehend least about the canine mind. Dogs need work and without labor they fall into trouble.

This dog, Ezra suspects, has a name, but not all animals do. The dog, of course, has a story. All animals do. Ezra walks up to the porch steps to look at him. He is neither a puppy nor old and he has not been neutered. Ezra does not gaze directly into the dog's eyes as he offers him his rolled fist to sniff. He studies his hand, before getting up to smell it. As the dog sniffs his fingers Ezra reaches his other hand into the pocket of his jacket for a treat.

"Hello," he says, withdrawing his hand to offer him the treat. The dog takes it and chews quickly. "Who are you?"

Closing his eyes, Ezra can see a crowded house in a frame of black and white images. The humans in the house are fighting. He can see a kick coming the dog's way and he sees "Boots," and lots of them.

"Boots," he says to the dog.

The dog looks comforted by the word and his name. Ezra sees a chain and a junkyard. Boots moves towards him and Ezra gently pats his head. The dog bumps into him and Ezra pets him even more. Boots wants to protect someone.

Ezra unlocks the front door. He holds it open so that Boots can make the choice. Boots looks into the house and then he goes up to Ezra and rubs his head against the veterinarian's thigh. Part of Ezra's professional demeanor slides. He rubs the big head of the animal. The dog licks his hand as the meowing of Horace Mann floats down the stairs from his position on the landing.

"Don't you dare, don't you dare," the cat tells him.

"Nice dog," Ezra says to Boots.

Boots smiles a big retriever grin, sloppy with great dollops of saliva.

Horace Mann chirps away at him "No, no, no," but Ezra remembers Daisy. He remembers their walks and his grandfather's pride in Ezra's ability with the Dalmatian, and he thinks what a handsome dog Boots is.

"Come and meet Boots" he calls to his wife.

"Ezra, Horace Mann is not going to like this," Anna says as she pushes the stroller to the porch.

"Horace Mann has an expansive heart. We have a big house. Maine coon cats are renown for living in homes with dogs."

These are all the statements that other veterinarians have made to Ezra about Horace Mann over the years. They think that Ezra needs to get over his desire to protect the big, marmalade-colored cat. "Horace Mann will thrive with another pet, Ezra," his partners tell him. But he has never taken their advice.

The dog walks into the house. Ezra closes the door and goes to meet Anna, lifting the now fussy Charlie out of the stroller. He smiles into the face of his wailing son.

"A boy needs a dog, Charlie," he says bouncing him.

"Don't you think we should discuss keeping a dog before we open the door and just let him in?" Anna says. "This dog is a stray. He's not neutered. He probably hasn't even had his shots. Dogs are not good with toddlers. He could go to a rescue group, Ezra."

"His name is Boots."

"And yours is James Herriot."

"I loved that show," he says, holding the door open for his beloved mate. Anna, he knows, takes on the characteristics of a small terrier when provoked.

"You and millions of cat-loving librarians."

"I love librarians."

Anna shakes her head.

"And I love one cat more than any other cat in the world, don't I, Horace Mann?"

Sleeping With Giraffes

KENNETH YELLOW DOG IS NOT LITTLE. As a child this was noted at every turn of his upbringing and education, kids being kids. Tall is tall. Kenneth is six-feet-five inches and he weighs two hundred and forty-four pounds. During the five years that Kenneth served in the United States Navy he spent a great deal of time ducking in and out of doorways whenever he was out to sea. Of course, he was not the only sailor with this problem. "Think of David Robinson" is the Navy lament for all tall sailors. David Robinson was too tall and never went to sea. He served his duty stateside as an engineer until he was mustered out and into the NBA. Kenneth is tall, but he was not too tall for the Navy. Most of the contemporary Yellow Dogs have served in the United States Navy and all of them are tall, and proud to be part of the color guard in any powwow's grand entry.

As a child growing up in Saint Francis on the Rosebud Reservation Kenneth loved playing basketball, as did his sister Clarice. Clarice was the better player of the two children, but this did not stop her brother from trying to beat her in a game of H.O.R.S.E. She is also a Chief Petty Officer in the Navy and the highest-ranking sailor of the extended Yellow Dog family. On the Rosebud Reservation it was expected that a boy as tall as Kenneth would play hoops, and he did. All of the boys and most of the girls in the small town of Saint Francis and on every reservation in the Dakotas played basketball, at least until they began to drink too much, or get into "other kinds of trouble" as Kenneth's mother always put it. Louise Freehold Yellow Dog, wife of Stanley Yellow Dog, worked as a kindergarten teacher at the Saint Francis Indian School. Louise says, "that kindergarten is the battlefield for hope" and "readiness for kindergarten is the blueprint for academic success." But don't get Kenneth's mother started on these topics. It is not that Kenneth doesn't completely agree with his mother and with the early childhood programming that public libraries are doing all over the United States, he does. It is just hard to get Louise to wind down once she has begun a stem-winder. Her voice goes up and up and dogs for miles around can hear her. It can be painful for canines. Even knowing this, Kenneth's mom cannot help spreading the word of her beliefs. Afterwards all she can do is ask the dogs for forgiveness. Louise's husband Stanley worked as a bus driver and a custodian for the school. That is how they met. It was in part an intersection of careers, but it was not only that.

Everyone on the reservation knew that the Yellow Dogs didn't drink. Many assumed it was because the family had converted to Mormonism. This was not the case. Or that Louise Freehold as a white woman made Stanley sign a religious pledge. Nor was this the reason. They avoid alcohol because it interferes with the gift that brought Louise and Stanley together in their later thirties when everyone thought that Louise was a spinster and Stanley a committed bachelor. She was a woman with an orange tabby cat and he was a man with a Lab-Sharpei mix dog. Both Kenneth and Clarice share this gift as well. The Yellow Dogs understand the feelings of animals. They can feel the pounding of their hearts and smell the anxiety of a creature's unhappiness. Sometimes they can outright hear an animal's thoughts, or see an image bouncing from dog to dog, or cat to cat. It is the same with wildlife.

"My dog Baxter told me that the new kindergarten teacher could understand him," Stanley told Kenneth and Clarice in explaining the genesis of their parents' courtship. "I didn't believe Baxter," their dad added after a pause. Then he laughed. "But that damn dog was right, and the kindergarten teacher was pretty."

"Watch your language, Stanley," Louise always adds, shyly, in the telling of their love affair.

Growing up, the Yellow Dog children ate a diet of beans, fry bread, and roasted root vegetables in the winter, and corn, tomatoes, beans, and fry bread in the summer. When a deer was hit on the roads coming into or going out of the village of Saint Francis, tribal police officers would call Stanley to come and claim the fresh kill. Road kill was accidental protein and always tasted of the freshness of a free life, or at least Stanley always maintained this. Kenneth liked the meals of venison; he still does. Clarice did not, but she would eat eggs from the chickens that Louise kept and drink milk from the family's various nanny goats. Around Saint Francis, and even at the Indian School the Yellow Dogs were considered good people, but odd. They were necessary employees in the running of the school, but they were moral to the point of being annoying — encouraging people to neuter their pets and grow their own food. This bugged folks who often could barely get by.

Dogs have always run wild on the reservation. Cats give birth to litter after litter, and then they die under the wheels of vehicles, or are eaten by coyotes. These are the plain facts of rural America. Stanley and Louise collected road kill and buried the bodies in an animal graveyard they kept on their property. The family sang hymns and read poems to these departed souls. Kenneth and Clarice made ceramic headstones from kits that Louise ordered through the mail. The fact that Louise Yellow Dog talked to her animals as she worked in the garden while listening to National Public Radio news shows and classical music on a transistor radio made her seem like a woman who aspired to be something greater. "And why shouldn't she?" some people said in her defense. "But they don't even have cable or a dish when they could afford it," people would say in response to that question. "And they don't drink." Or even worse, "Stanley's gone white."

Kenneth knows how brave his parents were in abstaining from drink. It is difficult to be sober and live on the Rosebud. The pain that his parents witnessed among the families they served until they achieved their respective retirements was very hard on them. Their conversations with the animals assuaged the Yellow Dogs' sense of helplessness in the face of the problems that the people of Saint Francis endured. Feeling what the animals felt and hearing what the animals said gave them something else to think about. Dogs and birds, cats and deer offered them something real and permanent while drink offered Louise and Stanley only a trip down a solipsistic hole with no help out of it. Alcohol strips something from their brains' neurotransmitters that leaves a Yellow Dog tone deaf to anything but his or her own thoughts. Kenneth tried drinking in the Navy, and it left him with no perception of what the seabirds were saying. The songs of the whales might as well have been Mandarin. He wrestled with many dark nights of the soul to regain complete sobriety as he finished his tour of duty because he liked drinking. It took months, half a year to stop. Too often he would slip off the wagon, drink pulling him downward and into a functional silent sadness where animals became incomprehensible creatures to him. Playing basketball helped him drink less and also the shrieks of a flock of seagulls that followed his carrier. These birds plagued his dreams, calling out to him from their beaks in English, "Kenneth, Kenneth come back to us," and he would awaken in sweats, praying that he would have the strength not to tip a few cold ones at the end of his day. In time the strength came.

The Yellow Dogs could smell the sadness and the fright in feedlot meat, but they also understood the terror of a rabbit taken by a red-tailed hawk. At night they would awaken to the screams of prey, small and tiny creatures calling out to be saved across the vastness of the land that is the Rosebud. By the time that Kenneth entered kindergarten he knew to say a prayer when a hawk was in the air. He neither found fault with the hawk nor assumed that in some way the rabbit would not be reborn.

As a tall little boy with a complete knowledge of sexual reproduction — the early scientific education of her children was something else that was held against Louise Yellow Dog — Kenneth considered what his cells had been before the sperm and ovum collided to become the fetal Kenneth in his mother's uterus. The sense of before and after is something that he pondered as he watched his father's gloved hands bury carcasses. He knew that the chemical properties of the soil and the creatures that lived within it would tear apart and re-use the tiny kitten and the abandoned yellow Labrador puppy that they were burying. The dead live on in worms and maggots and in the birds that tug these wriggling forms out of the earth's surface for food. His parents' cemetery was a springboard for life. Throughout the summer, bees, butterflies and hummingbirds hovered over the plants growing above the not forgotten dead. The flowers were lush in color and their fragrances filled both the day and the night with scent. Stanley and Louise Yellow Dog were careful to keep their animal graveyard quite separate from the family's vegetable garden. They taught Kenneth and Clarice never to touch dead animals with bare hands — lice, rabies, spongiform encephalopathy were health issues that they took seriously.

The Yellow Dogs do not speak openly of the family's gift. Nor do they assume that they are unique among the human species. Over the years they have all met others with similar abilities. Most likely a dog will mention it to them. Dogs are great talkers. Cats are more select in what they will reveal. Birds are gossips and sometimes inaccurate. Whales, elephants, and chimpanzees are holy and closest to the creator. Dragonflies are all about images and fireflies are frenetic, but to the point in their messages. Animals who herd or flock are far more similar to humans in thought than humans would want to consider. But people can be unpredictable, breaking with the crowd, cutting a new path, or changing their mind. In this way they are quite different from other living creatures. This characteristic makes it very hard for companion animals to predict human behavior, thus the need for training.

In the Navy, Kenneth and Clarice lived on ships with more people than they could have imagined as children on the reservation. Cats were the only animals on board, but it was rare for a Yellow Dog to converse with a cat. They earned their keep among the sailors by killing rats and mice and by making themselves scarce otherwise. While at sea the Yellow Dogs turned to other creatures for conversation. They were greeted by dolphins and heard the thoughts of terns and pelicans. They understood the vocalizations of whales. The worries of an albatross were the first communications that Kenneth understood as his body settled into two months of sobriety. He wept in joy and concern for these messages, feeling the bird's intense distress about the whirlpools of human trash destroying the oceans. When Kenneth remembers his time at sea, he says a prayer in thanks for his friends on board, in the oceans, and in the air, and for the healing powers of basketball.

Throughout his adult life Kenneth has played pick-up basketball. He loves the way a pick-up game can become the language between humans when no language is shared. The etiquette and energy of play can spell out a person's character; it can tell the story. Kenneth played pick up on ships in the Navy and with other sailors whenever they were in port. After his service he played intramural basketball while he attended Chadron State College. He joined playground games around Columbia when he studied library and information science at the University of Missouri. When Kenneth became manager of the Willa Cather Branch of the Omaha Public Library he continued to play with young men half of his age. He ignored his aching knees. Now he plays basketball at the Nebraska State Penitentiary when he has recreation time. His teammates, the opposition players, and the guards that patrol the games regard Kenneth

Yellow Dog as a skillful and gentlemanly player. He always gives voice to his admiration for a good play, even when it is against him. "Wow," he will say, or "Gosh darn, I didn't see that coming."

Most of Kenneth Yellow Dog's time is spent in the prison library, where he has been chosen to work as an aide. He and the prison librarian, Lionel Metcalfe, knew each other in graduate school. Theirs is an easy and respectful relationship based on the irony of who ends up behind bars. When Kenneth walks into the library he can see what Lionel needs him to do, whether it is shelving, dusting, or labeling the magazines and newspapers that the prisoners are allowed to read.

For the twelve years that Kenneth worked for the Omaha Public Library he was well liked by his fellow librarians. "Ken's incarceration is unfortunate," said his friend, retired rare books librarian Alfred Moorman to the *Omaha World Herald*, the paper of record for the State of Nebraska. Kenneth was renown among his colleagues for the Indian tacos he served at his Memorial Day potlucks and his volunteer work at the Siena/Francis House Homeless Shelter. In the same article, it was noted by librarian Madeleine Rea that, "Kenneth Yellow Dog is a deeply spiritual man. It would not be wrong to call Ken holy."

The talk among the staff at the library is that Kenneth might well be re-instated once he serves out his twenty-month sentence in Lincoln. The criminal lawyers in Omaha think he will be paroled months before that. There is a grim feeling about the situation at the Douglas County Courthouse because they prefer to prosecute bad guys, but it was still a win for them, all things considered. Zoo employees have been told not to speak to the media.

Anna Inwood, spokesperson for the library system, appears to be completely neutral on the topic of Mr. Yellow Dog's returning to the Omaha Public Library staff.

"Kenneth Yellow Dog's offenses had nothing to do with the library."

"Any further comments?" The media always persist in asking her.

"None," Anna will say.

Anna's reticence on the topic of Kenneth seems to indicate that the administration might well re-hire him. Far stranger things have happened in the city of Omaha. It is true that the patrons and staff love Kenneth. His prosecution has engendered support in a Free Kenneth Yellow Dog Facebook page, T-shirts, and a Kickstarter funding site that an intern for his lawyer created to help pay for his legal fees.

There is a felon or two in every family these days, or so his supporters say, and what Kenneth did hurt no one but himself. They believe that there are good felons and bad felons and that Kenneth Yellow Dog is a good felon. When Kenneth was found asleep among the giraffes at the Henry Doorly Zoo he left quietly when he was asked to do so by the zookeepers. The giraffes were agitated by Kenneth's leaving, and for days afterward took every chance that they could to spit on their keepers in ways that did not seem playful.

"Mr. Yellow Dog," they said, "You gotta go before the administrators get here."

"The giraffes wanted me to stay with them," he said from his curled up position on the building's floor. "They're my tallest friends."

This is true. Kenneth, like the nearly mute giraffes, is a man comfortable with his own silence and his height. Like these blond giants, Kenneth towers over his world. They have a view of the world that the close to the ground cannot comprehend.

The explanation was enough for the young employees of the zoo. All of them, at one time or another, had dreamed of sleeping among their favorite animals.

The second time Kenneth was found asleep among the giraffes he would not leave when he was asked and the administrators drove into work and found him sitting in the lotus position inside the giraffe house. They did call the Omaha Police who escorted him out of the zoo once they convinced him to leave the enclosure. As they handcuffed Kenneth the giraffes began to fling spittle onto the officers off of their long, blue and prehensile tongues. This was the beginning of his difficulties with Omaha's finest. Kenneth was then banned from entering the zoo, even though he was a long time member and donated to them every month out of a giving program at the library. His dad Stanley volunteered in the zoo's Diet Kitchen, and his mother Louise was a docent in the zoo's education programs. After Kenneth was removed by the police, zoo officials asked Stanley and Louise to take a sabbatical from their volunteering efforts.

Six weeks later staff found portions of the zoo's perimeter fencing severely compromised. A miniature donkey named Delilah was missing. Of course, parakeets, snakes, rabbits, small lizards, tarantulas, box turtles and several chickens and ducks had gone off the books over the years. This is not unusual in any zoo. Small creatures wander into the wrong enclosures and then larger and more predatory animals eat them. Or they slip outside of an exhibit space and are eaten by a fox or coyote, predators that are now part of urban wildlife. Birds fly away through tears in aviary screening to warmer climates in southern Missouri and Arkansas. Zookeepers know that they will lose small and feathered animals. They know that pigs will die in the barnyard display of viruses, or that after hours flamingoes and peacocks will descend into a lions' den or land in the polar bears' swimming pool to almost certain death. Wildlife will do what wildlife will do, but zoos don't advertise this reality to the public like they would the heart attack of a beloved gorilla or the passing of their last elephant. The nature that the zoo offers has always been rated PG, and it is carefully and sensitively orchestrated.

When the zookeepers could not find Delilah, not even her remains, it worried them. "Where did Delilah go?" they asked themselves. This was the question the public asked them, too, and many times a day, for they loved the little donkey. The growing concern about the missing miniature donkey among regular visitors led to a media release by the zoo officials, offering a reward for anyone knowing the whereabouts of Delilah. Her sweet image was on the front page of the *Omaha World Herald* and on *The Daily Nonpareil* in Council Bluffs. Omaha's television stations covered the story because it was a slow news day. Amateur sleuths all over Douglas County took it upon themselves to discover her whereabouts. And, of course, there was the reward to consider.

Kenneth Yellow Dog knew it was the police when he heard the knock on the front door from the backyard. One of the neighbors must have reported them is what he thinks as he re-shelves books for Lionel. It is quiet in the prison library. A very young looking man with badly done prison tattoos on each of his arms is reading the Bible. A middle-aged prisoner is reading Zane Grey's *Riders of the Purple Sage*. Kenneth has noted that a few prisoners are steady readers of westerns. They love Zane Grey and Louis L'Amour. Westerns, Kenneth thinks, speak to prisoners of freedom in isolated places where they might play out their stormy feelings and possibly do some good while not getting into trouble. One prisoner named Samuel Dent has been doing a great deal of research in support of his idea that NASA should send lifers into deep space as secret voyagers for the United States government. When not working on his NASA proposal Samuel Dent reads old science fiction novels. He loves Ray Bradbury and Robert A. Heinlein. Sam does not like L. Ron Hubbard. "The man wrote trash," he has told both Lionel and Kenneth, twirling his index finger around at his temple. "And he was crazy." Sam shot a man while robbing a gasoline station. The man lived. "Thank God," Sam always says about this part of his crime.

The weather was great that afternoon. Kenneth and his parents were in the backyard of his house on Webster Street with the animals. The yard was filled with blooming peony bushes and lilacs. When he heard the knocks on the door he walked around to the front of the house and said to the two police officers on the porch,

"May I help you?" as he would at the library.

"We are looking for Kenneth Yellow Dog."

"That is I."

"Is that you?"

"Yes."

"We have a search warrant."

They showed him the paper.

"Are you looking for Delilah?"

"The donkey."

"Follow me," he told them.

His parents were sitting in red Adirondack chairs. At his father's side was a rescued golden retriever mix whose fur was black except for a white patch on his chest. The dog's name is Panda. In his mother's lap was a rescued Persian cat name Golightly. Kenneth watched the police as they observed his parents petting the dog and the cat. Stanley and Louise were grinning as they watched Delilah the miniature donkey stand with the rescued miniature horses Hortense and Frida. The three tiny animals were eating the lawn's organically maintained clover. Even remembering this moment brings Kenneth sadness and pain, and a longing for his yellow bungalow on Webster Street.

Miniature donkeys are herd animals. Delilah had lost her partner Daniel earlier in the year and all of the Yellow Dogs understood her distress. She missed Daniel and she had fallen out of favor with the other creatures in the barnyard display. (Animals can choose to be deliberately nasty to one another. This is something that the Yellow Dogs understand and scientists have only begun to fathom.) Delilah was extraordinarily happy on Webster Street. Hortense and Frida, who are elderly miniature horses with big hearts, had taken in the grieving donkey. Beyond the tiny equines was a goat named Sally. Three hens named Jane, Patty, and Laura, and a rabbit named Dennis, were going in and out of the peony bushes. All of these creatures began their lives at the zoo. Each left as a juvenile in the pockets or lunch pails of either Stanley or Louise Yellow

Dog. None of the animals protested when they were moved. All of them had communicated a request for a change of venue to Kenneth's mom or dad. So his parents took them. No one pays attention to old white women schoolteachers or wrinkled Indians of any tribe, Kenneth thinks, as he puts the copies of *Time Magazine* in date order on the library's metal shelving. His mom's transistor radio was playing Antonin Dvorak's Symphony No. 9 in E Minor, "From the New World," as the two Omaha Police officers watched the bucolic scene in the Yellow Dog backyard. KVNO loves to play that symphony. If he ever hears it again outside of a penitentiary Kenneth knows he will weep.

"It looks like a scene from a movie," said the cop, holding the search warrant.

"Those are my parents," Kenneth remembers saying with pride to the police officer, as he sees his cellmate walk into the library. Kenneth was taller than both of the police officers. It was something that the officers noticed immediately about him from the front porch. Kenneth felt them making mental notes, sizing up the big Indian's temperament, wondering what he might do if they tried to arrest him. Being taller is intimidating and it is something that comes in handy in prison as it does in playing basketball. Other prisoners are afraid of him and his silence, of what he might do or what he knows. Some of the young felons who know a little about his crime think he is a freedom fighter for PETA, but they don't even know what the acronym PETA stands for, or the group's mission. Other guys think he played college basketball and then played on one of the traveling Native American teams. They call them Indian hoops. Kenneth did not, but he neither affirms nor denies. Mystery is helpful in prison.

"I was in the Navy," he will tell them if asked. "I worked as a librarian."

"Honorable discharge?"

"Honorable discharge."

"Go to college?"

"I went to college and graduate school."

"What's graduate school?"

"It's beyond college. I have a master's degree in library and information science."

"Shit, you gotta to be kidding. What the hell are you doing here?"

The police asked questions as well.

"Who took the donkey?" the cop who was not holding the warrant
asked.

"I did."

Both of the officers looked at him uncertainly.

"They're my parents. I love them," Kenneth said, answering a question that the police never asked.

The police called the zoo. When the zoo staff walked into Kenneth's
backyard they wanted to take Delilah and the chickens, the goat, and the
rabbit, as well. However the zookeepers had no proof that the other animals belonged to the zoo. No missing animals reports, just Delilah's.
Provenance, it turns out, is everything in both art and in animal heritage.
The Yellow Dog parents maintained a stoic silence. Louise Yellow Dog
did glare at the young woman who crated the bawling Delilah. When
Hortense and Frida began to whinny pitiful and ancient sounding cries
of concern for the donkey Stanley's eyes blinked with the energy and
rapidity of a person holding back tears.

Then the police handcuffed Kenneth and Louise shrieked, "No,"
as KVNO began to play Richard Strauss's "Thus Spake Zarathustra"
through her radio.

"Mom," Kenneth remembers saying. "It's okay. It's their job."

It all seems so stupidly apt to him that he is in prison for the theft
of a donkey that he didn't even like that much and that he didn't even
take or want. Delilah was a bit of a whiner as many herd animals are.
Quickly it all grew much more serious then Kenneth could ever have

imagined.

The police searched his house. They found the wire clippers that his dad had used to break in and rescue Delilah from the zoo. Then it turned out that Hortense and Frida were not from a rescue group as his parents had told him. They brought the little horses along with Panda and Golightly when they moved to Omaha from Saint Francis. Hortense and Frida had been reported stolen in Rapid City.

"You're saying that you did that, too?" his cousin Cameron Kills Pretty Enemy asked in a whisper when he interviewed him at the Omaha jail. "You live in Omaha. You couldn't have stolen those damn little horses in Rapid City. On the day that they were stolen you were clocked in at your library. People have come forward to say that they worked that day with you. Patrons have reported that you helped them."

"Look, Cameron, they're my parents. My dad has diabetes and he goes to dialysis twice a week. My mom," Kenneth paused. He didn't want to explain his complicated and wonderful mom to his cousin, who probably thought she was annoying, if not crazy. "Well, my mom is my mom."

"None of this makes sense," Cameron said, looking a bit disgusted. "Why are these two old people stealing animals?"

There was no way that he could explain to his cousin that his parents kidnapped animals because the animals told them they were unhappy. The one thing that Kenneth understands about Cameron Kills Pretty Enemy is that Cameron has never communicated with anything other than the human species and then only on his terms. Kenneth knows that Cameron would have called it "the Doctor Doolittle defense," and he just did not want to go there with him.

Iris Murphy called him at the library with the name of a criminal lawyer to represent him. Iris is a public defender. Kenneth had canvassed neighborhoods with her for the Democratic Party. He is tall and she is small. When people opened their doors to them they were charmed by the contrast in the pair. Even the Republicans gave them two minutes before declining their leaflets.

"Listen, Kenneth, you need the best criminal defense," she said. "Judges respect this man."

"But, Iris, I can't afford him."

"He will cut his fee in half."

"But why?"

"He owes me some favors and I am calling them in."

"For me?"

"For you."

The lawyer saved him from being sent to South Dakota to stand for charges of breaking and entering and horse theft. The state dropped the charges for many reasons, but mainly because the woman who owned Hortense and Frida kept the little horses in her feces strewn trailer and was a well-known animal hoarder. The horses were returned to South Dakota, but they were given to a rescue group, not their owner. The City of Omaha Health Department was not pleased to have two retirees keeping a goat and chickens without permits. Permits were obtained. Before he reported to Lincoln, Kenneth built a chicken coop with the help of Alfred Moorman.

The zoo dug in on wanting Kenneth prosecuted.

His lawyer said, "Kenneth, if your parents did it I think that I can get the charges regarding the donkey dropped. The prosecutor, I think, would strike a deal for them, but the zoo will not let them drop the charges against you because of the giraffe incident."

Kenneth Yellow Dog knows that part of the problem is that he is tall and dark and an Indian. In Nebraska, Native Americans will always be Indians, frightening and intimidating to so many people. White people always think of themselves as the good guys and everyone else as the bad guys, or just not as good. What they really are is just sort of pink-colored and capable of wrongdoing as every other human being.

The other half of his problem is that the zookeepers could not figure out how Kenneth got into the giraffe barn and he won't tell them how he did it. He promised the giraffes that he would not tell this secret to the zookeepers. He is a man of his word. So in retaliation for sleeping with the giraffes they pressed charges of felony theft in regards to Delilah. It was a lower class of felony, but a felony nonetheless. Cattle feeders' associations, ranching groups, and horse owners sent letters to the court asking that the charges against Kenneth not be dropped. All of them take animal theft seriously.

"I cannot do that."

Even a few weeks in prison would kill Stanley Yellow Dog. Kenneth knows this, as does his sister Clarice. And Louise would so irritate the guards at the Nebraska Correctional Center for Women at York with her nervous bird-like chatter and her opinions that they would not be nice to her. The Yellow Dogs are people of freedom. They talk to animals. They talk too much, sometimes. Kenneth would never entrust his parents' lives to a deal with the prosecutor. He grew up on the Rosebud Reservation and it, too, was a kind of a deal with a prosecutor.

In Navy uniform, Clarice wept at his sentencing. The judge looked away. Madeleine Rea sobbed. He saw Iris Murphy in the back of the courtroom. She was dressed beautifully like a yellow bird and Kenneth could hear her thoughts as though she were a robin in his backyard, or one of the pigeons that greeted him daily outside of the Willa Cather Branch Library. "Stay strong, Mr. Yellow Dog," she said clearly to him. "You are caring for your parents." Iris Murphy understood his position.

And here he is serving his parents' time for crimes that were not really crimes in any moral sense. Kenneth Yellow Dog has never hurt a flea or killed a mosquito or cheated on his taxes. He still loves his tall friends, the giraffes.

Now he is a man of prayers. And he hates the Nebraska State Penitentiary and he hates this feeling of hate. It is horrible thing to be locked up and to be "the big gentleman Indian" to the other prisoners. He misses his house and his parents and fresh black coffee in the morning. He longs for Madeleine Rea, the love of his life. His sleep is interrupted by the sad whispers of the mice that he can hear at night and the sighs of the water bugs that move freely between the cells. The mice are not happy mice. Over and over again they tell him they want to leave the prison, but they don't know how to do that, even though, of course, they do. There are creaks and crannies all over the building that provide transit. These mice could escape any time. But they won't. Mice like easy access to food and water. Moreover, they love that the humans are suffering inside the prison walls. It is true. They see it as tit for tat. They have said as much to Kenneth Yellow Dog.

Within six weeks Kenneth will be released. He has stayed strong. But he worries about his cellmate Leonard Howard. Kenneth does not know what to do for him. Leonard is deaf, mute, brilliant, and probably very mean in a quite narrow and depressed way. He backed into a cop who was approaching the rear of his car and then sped away. The officer was badly injured. When the police found Leonard he was very drunk and driving without a license, something he had done many times. He was unrepentant at the trial and would not apologize in court for what he did. Now Leonard spends as much time as he can in the library researching and writing a long article that he wants to submit to the *Journal of Pension Economics and Finance* on the issue of America's aging population. People are outliving the actuarial calculations for their life spans and defined benefit plans. Their lives are siphoning off the profits from companies like The Principal in Des Moines where Leonard Howard once worked as an actuary. Kenneth and Leonard communicate via scribbled notes and some sign language that Kenneth has learned in the time of their incarceration together. Kenneth knows that once he is released from prison he will speak with his financial planner about some of the issues that Leonard has mentioned to him in the scraps of papers that they have passed back and forth to each other before falling asleep at night.

Of course, Leonard is dying. This worries Kenneth as well. He presumes that his cellmate has both cirrhosis of the liver and hepatitis C. It is something he saw growing up on the reservation. It is an endgame in the world of addiction and unprotected sex. Also Leonard knows things about other prisoners. Things he will not reveal to Kenneth. Kenneth realizes that the other prisoners have no idea how much Leonard keeps in his notes, or what a calculating man he is. Prisoners are wrong to think that size and strength will always overcome meanness and cunning.

As he pushes his book truck past the table where Leonard is seated Kenneth looks down as Leonard looks up. Written in pencil in large capital letters across the border of the yellow legal pad where Leonard makes his notes is the name **IRIS MURPHY**. Leonard covers her name with an index card. Kenneth looks away. They will both pretend that Kenneth didn't see what he saw.

But Kenneth Yellow Dog's heart beats faster as he moves on to the Fiction shelves with his book truck. He should not be in this prison, and there are so many images and sounds that he wishes he could wipe from his memory of his time in Lincoln. He knows he will never visit Nebraska's capital again. He did not want to see this woman's name, the only attorney who understood his predicament and truly cared, on any prisoner's yellow legal pad. Many prisoners are obsessed with women on the outside, or the weaker males in their midst. Their fantasies are too often either pornographically ludicrous, or brutal. They talk about what they will do with a wife or a girlfriend when they get out as if they are like a meal to be eaten. This is why Kenneth Yellow Dog always plays basketball. He does not want to hear the sexual musings of inmates as they cluster together during recreation time. In this way, Leonard Howard is like the other prisoners. Sometimes in his notes to Kenneth, Leonard writes statements about an ex-wife or a former girlfriend and what he writes is almost always disparaging in his characterizations of them. The anger in the notes disturbs Kenneth, but he does not find it unusual. Prison air is filled with anger. It hangs in oily mists among the men. What Kenneth doesn't breathe in he feels on the bare skin of his forearms. Anger has a stink all its own.

As he shelves the books of David Baldacci, Vince Flynn, Donald Goines, and Ernest Hemingway, Kenneth prays for Iris Murphy. Praying makes him feel like he is doing something to protect her. But from what, he does not know.

Kenneth straightens a shelf of John Grisham novels and then turns to reach for a handful of Jack Higgins paperbacks when he hears the scraping sound of a chair being pushed backwards. The plump sound of the thump of a body hitting the floor follows. A chair topples. A head smacks against the industrial linoleum that covers the library's cement floor.

"Ken, Ken," Lionel calls out to him.

Kenneth pushes aside the book truck and runs to where Lionel is. He sees Leonard flat on the floor and the prison librarian kneeling beside him, pressing down on his chest. The deaf actuary's gasps are audible and the fingers of his hands are flailing some incomprehensible message.

"Take over the CPR, Ken, while I get the guards," Lionel says, his voice shaking, as he stands up.

The other prisoners have moved to look at Leonard Howard's form crumpled next to the fallen chair. Blood seeps from his head where the skin parted as the cranium hit the flooring. Samuel Dent whispers the Lord's Prayer.

"Our Father who are in heaven, hallowed be thy name."

Folding his tall frame down to his knees, Kenneth begins the compressions. He looks into his cellmate's frightened eyes, and for the first time, he realizes that they are brown like a giraffe's and that Leonard, like those tall animals, was once a handsome creature. Leonard's moving hands brush against Kenneth's arms, telling him something, but Kenneth fails to comprehend the message. With each press of his folded hands to Leonard's chest he feels his cellmate receding.

"Come on, Leonard, come on," he shouts to the deaf man. "Fight for it."

But Leonard Howard fades. The light in his brown eyes is gone. He has left the library. Samuel Dent begins to sing "We Shall Overcome" as Kenneth Yellow Dog cries and the guards gather around them.

Desire, Fear, Shock,
and Awe

STANDING ON THE SIDEWALK Martha looks at Iris. Iris smiles at her and then turns her head to look for Paul who has stopped to use the restroom. It is cool outside of the restaurant and overcast. It was not the kind of day that Martha would have expected tornadoes for Omaha, but there is drama to a funnel cloud and humans are drawn to drama. Surrounding the two women are smaller groups of younger couples waiting for tables and teenagers dressed in shorts and sundresses who are eating ice cream cones as they walk through the neighborhood. Everyone seems to be carrying an umbrella while Martha is not. The teenagers are all beautiful and handsome in ways that they cannot know. The chatter of their voices and the sounds of their laughter almost bring Martha to tears. For them the night is young and they are rich in time. She reaches out to take Iris by the arm. Iris leans into her and Martha puts her other arm around her.

"Together, we have stood on this street corner for decades, Martha, dear," Iris says with a laugh, looking at the intersection of 50th Street and Underwood Avenue. "Remember the hip huggers of 1970? When my dad saw us walking to your house. He was on the fire truck going down Underwood Avenue screaming, 'Iris Bernadette Murphy, go home and put on some proper clothes.'"

Martha remembers. It was in 1970, after the Kent State shootings.

The President of the University of Iowa had closed the school because of the protests, so Martha packed her bags, as did all the girls at the Kappa Kappa Gamma House, and came home.

"Jack Murphy hated those hip huggers," Martha says, conjuring up in her mind Iris's dad, who frightened Martha in her girlhood with his gruffness.

"My dad hated everything in women's clothing styles except nun's habits."

"Jack would have loved the burqa."

Iris giggles. "The more he hated fashion the more I loved it."

"Girls, girls," Paul calls out as he walks towards them.

Martha hugs Iris and then she waves to Paul who is meandering through the chattering clumps of people. When he reaches them he asks,

"What's so funny?"

"We were just remembering how much my dad hated hip huggers."

Paul shakes his head. "Jack Murphy must have despised every moment of the sixties and the seventies. The clothes, the hair, the protests."

"Bridget and I wore our hair as long as possible," Iris says. "It clogged the drains of our bathroom sinks and the shower in the basement. Dad was forever unclogging them. When I was in seventh grade at St. Cecilia's, boys rode their bicycles up and down Webster Street past our house, screaming, 'I love you, Iris Murphy,' and that's when Dad decided that I had to go to Duchesne Academy."

"We had to lie down on a bed to zip up those hip huggers." Martha says, sighing. "I got my hair cut just like Jane Fonda. I wore Kohl under my eyes."

"One Saturday afternoon, unbeknownst to Dad, Bridget wore a bikini to the Elmwood Park swimming pool and the lifeguards had to call for an ambulance because someone slipped on the tiles in the changing room. Bridget Murphy's bikini was the talk of the fire house that whole summer and Dad told Mom that she was going to have to lock the two of us up and throw away the key."

"And here we are, so many years later, sedate as can be on Underwood Avenue," Martha declares, as they walk away from the restaurant and towards Iris' house. Pots of impatiens and geraniums hang from the lampposts. Bridal wreath bushes spill over with blooms in front of houses set back from the street. Lilacs scent the air. The residents of Omaha wander out of their homes and into the evening. They stand in their yards, eyes closed, faces towards the sky, relief in their sighs that the day of tornadoes has passed them by. The still overcast sky robs the fading sun of its spectacle. Even in the half-darkness the greenery of the trees and the heaviness of the spring flowers charge the atmosphere with a specific kind of beauty. Now, Martha thinks is now, holding onto Iris's arm. She will not contemplate Iris's cancer until she is alone. Martha likes to put the best face on things. She fears giving into emotions too quickly. "Panic never aids calamity" is what she tells her staff at the bank when they become overwhelmed by a problem. And she always adds, "Very little in life is true calamity."

"Hey, Paul, beautiful evening" a handsome, young man calls out to him.

"That it is, that it is," Paul says, smiling.

The three of them stop so that Paul can chat.

Martha feels how happy Paul is to draw the attention of a younger man. Paul may be madly in love with his new friend, but he still loves being noticed. Iris looks at the two men and stifles a giggle, squeezing Martha's hand. Paul turns back to them as his young friend walks on.

A woman walking a dog waves to Iris, and a colleague from the bank greets Martha as they turn south onto 50th Street. Martha Elizabeth Berger does not spend a great deal of time considering her past. The discussion of hip huggers is something Martha will do with Iris because Iris loves the sheen of memories. Iris can recall moments in their girlhood that Martha has long forgotten. She attends Duchesne Academy alumnae events with Iris, but she has never longed for yesterday. She doesn't even like the Beatles song of that title. Some of their classmates seem to yearn for the years when they were all in high school together. This point-of-view is something Martha attempts to respect when the topic comes up at luncheons, but it is not something she understands. How can a woman who has three children long for a time before a husband or her children? Even if they could live without the husband could they live without the children? Martha adores Miles Brendan Murphy, Iris's son, and she loves her brother Tom's daughters, Anna and Emma. She cannot imagine a world without Miles or her nieces. Their youth makes her age all the better. As Martha sees it, the whole purpose of education is to catapult forward from it, not to want to re-live it, as though life were an eternal do-over. It is why she always leaves alumnae dinners early so as to avoid the maudlin effects that a third glass of wine can offer. Too much wine leads to the discussion of former boyfriends and deaths. The past is past and it is as utterly unknowable as the future, because one never knows all of the events of any history, even one's own. Once Martha declared this sentiment to a lover and it sparked the argument that broke up the relationship.

When Martha was a child she longed for adulthood. In reality she felt that she was already an adult. Martha was never that interested in the children around her, except for her brother Tom and a little girl named Susan who lived down the block.

Her mother, Rita, often used to shake her head and say, "Martha, you popped out of my womb forty-years-old."

However, the idea of three glasses of wine begins to appeal to Martha as darkness descends on the city and the person she would love to drink them with is Paul. But Paul cannot drink because he is a man in recovery who will never be recovered and that is the irony of twelve-step programs. Iris is what she and Paul share and there are things that only Paul can understand. Usually Martha would drink the wine with Iris, pouring out her heart to her friend's sympathetic ears, and spending the night in Iris's spare bedroom if she takes the third glass. What Martha wants to say to Paul and to the world, with or without the wine, is that she has never imagined a life without Iris.

From the moment Martha saw Iris standing in the Duchesne Academy parking lot in 1964, she knew that this girl was going to be her friend. Martha was perched on the steps of the terrace that led up to the Foxley Building, waiting to meet up with some girls from Saint Margaret Mary School, when she watched Iris walk into the parking lot. Iris was wearing an oversized, hand-me-down, pink shirtwaist uniform and her hair was in two long black braids down her back. Following Iris was a woman in a white uniform like the maids wore who worked in the houses in Martha's neighborhood. Martha would see these women waiting at the bus stops on Dodge Street when she walked home from elementary school. Holding onto the woman's hand was a younger girl, with the same kind of braids, who was crying. Iris handed the pile of books and notebooks that she was carrying to the woman and began to sign to the silent, sobbing girl. The younger girl's hands flew in response. Finally Iris wrapped her arms around the child, rocking her back and forth and kissing her cheeks and the top of her head. Walking around this impassioned yet silent tableau were all the older girls who wore their hair in bouffant hairdos. As privileged juniors and seniors they could smoke the first cigarette of the day in public and then toss it with a studied nonchalance to the parking lot's asphalt surface while trying not to look at the little freshman and her sobbing sister.

What stood out to Martha is that Iris did not seem to care what all the other girls thought as they were striding past her. She did not shoo her family away like Martha would have done if they had brought her to school that very first morning of freshman year. After the rocking and kissing and some more signing the younger girl smiled, letting go of Iris to grab the woman's skirt. The woman in white kissed Iris on the forehead, whispering something into her ear before handing her the stack of books. Then hand-in-hand the woman and the girl watched Iris, with her head bowed and her body swallowed up in her pink uniform, march alone past the small groups of freshman girls in the parking lot and up the terrace stairs, brushing Martha with the swish of her long skirt and into the school. Without a word Iris Murphy declared herself to the world of the Sacred Heart.

The nuns grew to love Iris very much and the other girls did not resent Iris for this fact, because they knew that the nuns loved them all, but more to the point, the girls at the school did not want to be Iris. Iris was pretty enough, but not nearly as pretty as some of the other girls at Duchesne Academy who were, quite honestly, breathtakingly beautiful. Nor was Iris as educated as the girls from the better parish schools like Saint Margaret Mary's or Christ the King, but she was smart and she caught on quickly to what the teachers wanted. What the girls realized is that Iris was different from them, and they would not want her differences. Her father was a fire fighter and her mother worked as a baker. Iris's sister was deaf and the whole family talked with their hands, saying words that could only be imagined by those who could hear. To Iris's classmates it all looked like a world of work, effort, and quite strange, but they were, in general, kind girls, brought up by their mothers to live by the dictum, *If you can't say something nice then you needn't say anything at all.*"

Martha could attest to the fact that Iris always worked. She worked as a portress for the nuns and also on the counter at the bakery where her mother made the cakes. Later she was an admissions escort at Clarkson Hospital and after that she got on with Mutual of Omaha as an evening filing clerk. In college, Iris was a page for the Omaha Public Library. Throughout high school, Martha remembers a look of weariness on Iris's face, especially during morning homeroom, but that she never complained.

Three weeks into freshman year Martha invited Iris to spend the night. She watched Jack Murphy park his truck and walk his daughter up the sidewalk to the front door. Next to her handsome father, who was wearing his firefighter's uniform, Iris seemed even smaller. The doorbell rang and Martha's mother answered the door.

"Hello, Jack Murphy."

"Good evening, Rita O'Toole."

As the adults exchanged pleasantries, Iris walked into the living room with her pajamas and toothbrush in a paper Brandeis bag.

Martha said to her, "They know each other?"

"My dad knows everybody in Omaha."

On Sunday, after Iris had gone home, Martha cornered her mother in the kitchen as she was putting a roast beef in the oven.

"You didn't tell me you knew Mr. Murphy."

"I have known Jack Murphy since first grade. He's Irish and I'm Irish and that's that. His mother sang in the choir at the Cathedral. We all knew each other then."

"But you didn't tell me."

"Do you want to know about everyone in my first grade class?"

What Martha wanted to say was that Jack Murphy was handsome, but she felt that it would be disloyal to her father, who was watching a football game on the television in the sunroom, to put those words into the universe. Martha's father was kind and roly-poly and her mother was forever putting "the whole family on a diet" to help him lose weight. Her mother was beautiful. Men looked at her when the family was out in public.

Martha had never imagined her mother marrying anyone but her father until she met Mr. Murphy. What puzzled Martha was the notion of attraction. Was her mother as attracted to her father, as her father was attracted to her mother? She wanted to ask her mom if she had ever been attracted to Mr. Murphy, but her mother was already out of the kitchen, up the stairs and in her bedroom to read the Sunday paper and nap, an inviolable ritual. Attraction was the mystery of Martha's life.

Although the nuns emphasized education and college, mothers emphasized finding "the right boy and the right type of marriage." Mothers wanted girls well prepared for matrimony to men who would be "going places." "Going places," as Martha remembers it, was the Omaha euphemism for making money.

Men like Jack Murphy were going to union halls after their shifts at the firehouse. On his days off, Jack installed HVAC equipment which Martha came to learn meant "Heating, Ventilation, and Air Conditioning." Jack saw no reason why his wife should not work as a baker, if he could be home to watch the girls when she was gone. Honora Murphy, it appeared, agreed with this point-of-view. Mrs. Murphy was a fine baker and she taught that skill to both Iris and Bridget.

"I love Iris Murphy to death," Rita Berger told 16-year-old Martha, as she drank a third glass of Mateus Rose late one Saturday evening. "But I'm thrilled that she's not a boy. You would probably fall in love with any son of Jack Murphy's, if he had a son."

Everything that every mother worried about in 1964 did happen and the earth went right on spinning and life did not stop in Omaha, or anywhere else. Martha often thinks of this when she visits her mom. Goodness in its human components continued and as did the wretched aspects of its opposite as well. God threw no known thunderbolts, at least, none that were reported in the *Omaha World Herald,* the day Martha walked into Planned Parenthood during the summer of 1969 for her just-in-case birth control. The sky was equally calm the morning she registered as a Democrat in 1976.

Rita O'Toole Berger has been widowed for fifteen years. She lives in the Elmwood Tower. Martha calls her mother every day and visits her three or four times a week, as she did today. They spent the afternoon knitting, ignoring the dark and overcast sky, and listening to opera on public radio. She does not know how she will tell her mom about Iris's diagnosis. Her mother will howl with indignation, angered by the capriciousness of a God, who would do this to little Iris. Colon and liver cancer have little to do with God, Martha knows, and everything to do with the multiplication of the wrong kinds of cells, but Rita will have none of this kind of talk. The closer her mother grows to death the more she has to tell to God. "The old should die," she tells Martha at least once a week, "so that the young can get on with things."

Martha does not want her mom to die anymore than she wants Iris to die. She blinks back tears at the notion of their passing and she prays silently to a God that she has ignored for decades, most often while in church, to heal Iris and to keep her tart-tongued Mother alive and well enough in her two bedroom apartment in the Elmwood Tower.

Lately, Rita Berger has taken up the truth, at least the truth as Rita sees it.

"We all had a crush on Jack Murphy," she told Martha, one day over a Lenten lunch of grilled cheese sandwiches and tomato soup. "He was handsome, brave and courageous even in first grade. How can you not love a firefighter? Even thinking about him made me long for a cigarette. But think of how hard Honora Murphy worked, Martha? I couldn't face all that work, sending Bridget away to boarding school and then Bridget married the Negro man and Iris had the baby out-of-wedlock. Oh, it all seemed so horrible and lower class and scandalous then. But it all worked out. So there you have it. What did I know? Wasted worry is what that was."

"But you loved, Dad, right?" Martha had to ask, even at 62-years-of-age, out of loyalty to her father.

"Of course, I loved your father. How could I not love your father? But don't you love George Clooney, dear? Isn't there always a secret someone in a woman's heart?"

Mrs. Berger is madly in love with George Clooney.

"Martha," Iris says, stopping on the sidewalk two blocks from her house, interrupting Martha's rush of unexpected memories.

"Pardon me?"

Martha looks at Iris and then at Paul.

"I just said, 'Could you stop for one moment?' There's something that I need to tell you and Paul."

The three of them are alone on the sidewalk. They can see Iris's house. The porch light glows over the front door. No cars are moving on the street.

"I don't think that I mentioned to the two of you that I had a letter from Leonard Howard."

"Who's he?" Paul asks.

"You didn't respond to him?" Martha blurts out, knowing that she should listen, but she cannot stand Leonard Howard. Leonard is a handsome, troubled and careless man. He is worse than the cancer buried in Iris's colon and liver.

"I did," Iris says.

"Oh, Iris, why?"

Martha knows that she is being callous, but Leonard is such a difficult man and he was an arrogant boy. She knows that Iris wants her to feel some kind of sympathy because of Leonard's deafness, but a shit is a shit and that is all that she can think, even now. Leonard always treated Iris with a kind of ownership, his arm around her, pulling Iris back from her friends the summer that he dated her while they were in high school. He always looked at Martha and the other girls from Duchesne with contempt. Martha didn't have to be able to interpret American Sign Language to know that Leonard didn't like her. The look of antipathy spreading across a face is a universal human expression. Even years after he broke up with Iris, Leonard would turn up in Omaha bars and upon seeing Iris ignore her greetings, leaving Iris in tears and Martha enraged. Leonard hurt Iris to create hurt.

"Leonard asked me to visit him at the prison. He sent me the paperwork."

"Who the hell is Leonard?" Paul interjects into the conversation.

"Iris's high school boyfriend who was arrested for backing into a police officer after being stopped for drunken driving," Martha says, answering the question. "The police officer was badly injured. Leonard sped away, leaving him on the side of West Dodge Road. Iris told you about it."

"Oh," Paul says in a noncommittal fashion, as he always does when he knows more, but will not say, because he is a member of Alcoholics Anonymous. "Now I remember him. Terrible situation."

"I visited Leonard at the State Penitentiary in Lincoln," Iris says.

"Why would you do that?" Martha asks her, hearing a note of real anger in her own voice.

"Martha," Paul says. Martha hears caution in his tone.

"I'm almost sixty-four years old," Iris says. "I loved Leonard once. At seventeen, I dreamed of marrying him and then he dropped me like a hot potato. He never spoke to me again. I wanted to know why he did that before ..." and then Iris stops.

Martha feels like a bitch as she always does when she interrogates Iris about a failed relationship. Iris has never had timing or luck in love. But Iris has not dated anyone for over a decade and Martha dreads the idea that she might become involved with a prisoner. It would destroy her legal reputation. The Omaha police would never forgive a public defender for dating someone who had so callously injured a cop.

"I'm sorry," Martha says. She wants to get her apology out in the open, before Paul chides her, or Iris begins to cry.

But Iris is already crying.

"You're right, Martha, you've always been right about Leonard Howard. He has never loved me and he is a very troubled man, but ..."

"What, Iris, what?" Paul says, looking at Martha with eyebrows raised.

Iris has begun to sob. Martha puts her arms around her and feels a sense of terror. Iris can sometimes be teary, but she has never sobbed, not even when her parents died. Paul looks up and the down the street, aware as Paul always is, that someone might be watching them, but Martha sees no one.

"Tell us, Iris," he says. "What's wrong?"

"Leonard can read lips," Iris says, her eyes moving from Martha to Paul. "The other prisoners don't know this and neither do the guards. He has learned to interpret the signs the prisoners use to confuse the guards. There is a prisoner who talks about me. Leonard has read his lips. He understands the signs."

Martha pulls Iris closer to her. She feels Iris shake and then shudder, "Iris, Iris," she coos to her. "Everything will be okay."

"What did Leonard learn?" Paul asks, in a serious, quiet tone.

"There is a prisoner who hates me. A prisoner named Angelo Bartlett who wants to get even with me. I'm afraid of going home."

"I want you to spend the night at my place," Martha says.

"But," Iris says.

"No buts," Paul tells her firmly. "I've told you for years to sell that house. It's too big for one person. You can get a condo with plenty of room for Miles.'

"You're a public defender, Iris," Martha finds herself saying with a note of anger in her tone. "Sixty percent of all the impoverished felons in the Omaha metro area know you. It wouldn't take much for them to find your house."

"I'm unlisted."

"Iris, they can find you on the Internet," Paul says.

"They could follow you home from the courthouse one night," Martha adds. "Paul and I have been telling you this for years."

"But I love the house."

"We know that, Iris," Paul says very gently.

"Please, please stay with me tonight, Iris."

Iris nods her head and the three of them pivot in the direction of Martha's place and ten minutes later they are there. It is a small brick house tucked between two larger Dundee homes.

"I will be in touch," Paul says, after he kisses Iris and then Martha on the cheek and then he hurries away, presumably, Martha thinks, to his new gentleman friend.

Pooh Dog runs around the women's legs as they walk in the door, barking his greeting.

"Settle my sweet Pooh, settle," Martha says to him, refusing to pet the apricot-colored toy poodle until he has taken a seated and silent position on the floor.

Martha then closes the door and pets the dog.

"Might I have a glass of wine, Martha, dear?"

"Why not two?" Martha says in reply after she kisses Pooh Dog on his head.

"I need to use the bathroom," Iris says, almost shyly.

"Please do."

"May I borrow some pajamas while I'm up there?" Iris asks, looking toward the staircase to the second floor. "Put them on, I mean."

"Of course. You know where they are."

"Should I wear Laura's?"

"No, you can wear a pair of mine," Martha says, knowing that Laura will sense if someone has worn her pajamas. Over the years the guestroom has become Laura's. Martha's lover notices even slight changes in the hangers in her closet, or the layout of hand and facial creams on the bathroom vanity when she visits from Denver.

"Thank you," Iris says.

"It's nothing," Martha tells her.

"It's everything," Iris replies, as she makes her way up the stairs.

Martha lights the candles in the front room of her house and puts kibble in Pooh Dog's dish and then lets him out the back door into her fenced in yard to do his business. She opens the front room windows and smells the evening. When Iris returns she is in an old pair of Martha's pajamas. They are pink flannel. She has rolled up the pant cuffs and the sleeves of the shirt. Iris's small feet are bare. Her toenails are painted a fuchsia color. Martha smiles. Iris loves adornment.

Martha hands her a glass of chardonnay saying, "I forgot all about those pajamas. They are relics of my ancient history."

Iris sips the wine, grinning.

"Thank goodness it's buttery. I know I'm supposed to hate oaky wines, but I don't. It dates me to the 1990s, I'm sure."

Martha laughs. This is why she loves Iris. Iris never pretends.

"Is it okay if we talk about Angelo Bartlett and the house tomorrow?"

"Yes, but I want you to know that I think you should sell the house."

Iris nods her head.

"And get a dog."

"I love you, Martha."

"I love you, Iris."

Then the two women curl up, each in her corner of the old floral sofa that Martha brought from her parents' house. They silently sip wine. Martha can hear the chirrup of crickets in the grass. The candles flicker. Her toe touches the thick carpet beneath coffee table. Art books are piled beneath the glass top of the table. Martha is happy to be quiet with Iris. Laura is all noise and activity when she flies in from Denver for their weekends together. She fills up the house, her arm always around Martha, stealing kisses and copping feels. Even at the Kappa Kappa Gamma House when Laura was pinned to Tom Juergens, Martha would look up to find Laura staring at her. The first time Laura kissed Martha she was wearing the diamond engagement ring that Tom had given her. The ring scratched Martha's cheek as Laura grabbed her face to pull her close.

Everything about Laura Heard is large. She towers over Martha in the stiletto heels she continues to wear. Her hair was longer and blonder than any other girl's in the Kappa house. It is shorter now, but not by much, and just as blonde. Her deep, husky voice commands attention. From her friends she has always demanded loyalty, but from Martha she demands fealty. Even as she prepared to marry Tom, Laura sought out Martha, taking her to every lonely spot in Iowa City, from graveyards to the sides of deserted county roads, where she kissed Martha into submission in the back seat of her pink Camaro.

"You're besotted with that foolish girl," Rita Berger would say when Laura's telephone calls would come into Omaha at midnight during the summer breaks.

Laura was three months pregnant with Tom's baby when they married two weeks after graduation. Martha was one of the five sorority sister bridesmaids at their nuptials in Denver's Cathedral Basilica of the Immaculate Conception. The wedding broke Martha's heart. When Martha returned from the event Iris picked her up at the Eugene C. Eppley Airport in Omaha. For two hours, Iris drove Martha around the city so that she could shed all of her tears before going home to her parents.

After Laura, Martha never again looked at men, but she began to notice women like herself and where they spent time in Omaha. An acquaintance invited her to a lesbian event in Chicago. It was Iris who told her to go. Martha did and something inside her began to blossom. There she reconnected with a friend from Iowa City who lived in Des Moines. Only Iris knew that Martha and the woman were lovers, holding hands at lesbian gatherings and dancing salaciously in the few gay bars of Des Moines. But Laura still called Martha in the middle of the night and Martha still took her calls until a gauntlet was thrown down.

"You spend too much time with Iris Murphy," Laura said.

"I love Iris Murphy."

Martha said this without thinking.

"You can love me or Iris Murphy.'

"Then I choose Iris."

Laura slammed the phone down. They did not speak for three years.

Martha sips her wine and looks at Iris who is looking across the room. The truth is that she has always loved Iris Murphy. Even now when she and a twice-divorced Laura are once again seeing each other Martha continues to love Iris. Martha closes her eyes.

"Martha, I need to tell you something."

"What is that Iris?"

"I have a limited amount of time."

Martha opens her eyes. Her heart is beating rapidly. She takes a big drink of the chardonnay.

"You have to give the oncology a chance, Iris."

"I have decisions to make about oncology."

Iris says this in her courtroom voice. Martha has heard it before. She sighs.

"Oh, Iris."

"Now you must listen to me, Martha, dear," Iris says, putting her empty wineglass on a coaster in the center of the glass of the coffee table and standing up.

"I always listen."

Iris walks down to the end of the sofa and sits next to Martha. She takes Martha's glass of chardonnay and puts in on a coaster next to her own. She takes both of Martha's hands in her hands. She looks like child in her pink flannel pajamas.

"Martha, I love you."

"Thank you, Iris."

Iris shakes her head.

Martha looks into Iris Murphy's blue-gray eyes. She sees solemnity. She sees earnestness. Her heart beats.

"Martha, I love you, and when Laura is not here I want to be your lover. It is what I want to do with my time."

"What about the men in your life?"

Iris winces.

"Am I going to be your hobby?"

Even Martha can hear the raw jealousy in her voice. There have always been men in Iris Murphy's life. And Martha has always been jealous of them.

Iris moves in closer. The soft flannel of the pajamas rubs against Martha's shoulder where her sweater has slipped away from her spring dress. Iris kisses the palms of Martha's hands. She pushes up the soft sleeves of Martha's sweater to kiss her forearms. She kisses her elbows, her shoulders, and her neck and then pulls back to gaze into Martha's eyes. Her eyes are unwavering in their seriousness.

"You are what I want, Martha."

Shaking with desire and fear, Martha Berger pulls Iris Murphy into her lap and then she kisses her best friend's lips. She feels shock and awe when Iris kisses her in return with an open mouth and a full tongue, her arms locking around Martha's neck in a fierce hug. They are crying and kissing as Martha unbuttons the pink flannel pajamas and reaches into them. With her white-hair gleaming in the candlelight, Iris strips off the pajamas and straddles Martha. She kisses her with such a force that Martha feels the earth tilt towards the moon and the ice on her heart breaks loose.

Pooh Dog begins barking somewhere in the background. It is Iris who walks through the shadowed kitchen to let him in. Martha blows out the candles and leads her best friend up the stairs and into her bed, shutting the door to bar the dog and the world.

Iris winces as she slides under the duvet. Martha reaches for Iris, hoping to kiss her and make the boo-boo of cancer somehow better. Iris looks at her and Martha sees steadiness in her eyes beyond the pain.

"It is what it is, my love," Iris says.

Martha's hands find her friend's warm, small breasts, and her lips Iris's lips. Iris swoons. She clings to Martha as if to dear life.

Kills Pretty Enemy

MILES MURPHY UNLOCKS THE SAFE ROOM of his apartment in Nairobi. For him the space has none of the easeful comforts of a bedroom, but it is where he sleeps and where he communicates with the world outside of Kenya. Inside the room he closes the door, locking it. Sitting down at his desk he opens his laptop and types in the password. Out of habit he calculates the time difference between Omaha and Kenya as he logs onto Skype, waiting for his mother to do the same. Miles tends to be early, his mother tends to be breathlessly on time, as though she is late, but she never is. As he waits for her he checks his email and Facebook. His BlackBerry buzzes. He pulls it out of his pocket to stare at it. It is someone selling something that is nothing. So much, he thinks, is nothing.

At night when Miles is tired, and he knows that he must go to sleep, he unlocks the room at the back of the apartment to lock it again after he has entered. Then he plugs his BlackBerry into the surge protector and puts his wallet into the middle drawer of the desk. Once he has gotten between the sheets and taken off his eyeglasses, putting them on a small table beside the bed, Miles says his prayers with his hands, in American Sign Language, as his mother taught him to do. First, he prays for the world and then for his family, and friends, and, finally, for himself, before his eyes close to the hum of a ceiling fan.

Next to the sleeping room is the bathroom. Waking up in the wee hours of the morning to take a leak is always a hassle; beer is often the culprit for this inconvenience. In the middle space, away from his small kitchen and dining table, but before the sleeping room are a bookcase, a couch facing the apartment's singular grilled window, a small, high definition television, and a set of weights stacked on a rack beneath the window. Miles thinks of this area as the Free Land. He reads on the couch in the Free Land, lifts weights, or watches sports on the television there before he locks himself away at night. The series of locks on both sides of the door are strong and serious. The door itself is nearly impenetrable. When things go wrong in Nairobi they go wrong quickly. As a firefighter in Omaha, his grandfather, Jack Murphy, hated excessive locks in residential buildings, especially locks that needed keys. Only in movies is it easy to kick open a locked door. It takes axes, strength, and long seconds to break down doors when a building is burning.

"In a fire, people die at the damn door because the key isn't close enough to the dead bolt. They panic because the smoke makes it impossible for them to find the damn key and then the smoke asphyxiates them while they search."

Grandpa Jack would have howled at the sight of the locks in his grandson's apartment in Nairobi. Daily the keys and the bolts remind Miles of his grandfather who worried about candles, smoking in bed, and people unable to escape from their burning homes. Grandpa Jack only smoked when he sat in front of the fire station or when he mowed the lawn or shoveled snow. He loathed bad wiring. Tools were his gift of choice for Miles's birthday or Christmas presents. By the time that Miles entered Lewis & Clark Middle School he had built a tree house with his grandfather and helped to remodel the basement of their home on Cass Street. Building things, like bookcases, and putting together the cheap but often complicated furniture that Foreign Service employees always need, comes naturally to Miles. He is known for being willing to help newcomers at the embassy move into their apartments and always

Kills Pretty Enemy

ready to cook for a potluck. When Miles began college at the University of Nebraska in Lincoln he could make six different kinds of prizewinning chili; he learned to cook and clean at the fire station. Some of his former girlfriends joked about his neat apartment, as though men are supposed to be slobs. Their humor hurt his feelings, but he would never admit it. Miles connects order and cleanliness to masculinity.

Margaret D'Souza has never said a word about the interior of his apartment and this is just one of the many qualities that Miles loves about his girlfriend. It is one of the things that he wants to tell his mom as they Skype, but first he needs to tell his mom that he is dating Margaret D'Souza and that it is serious. Around the embassy Miles and Margaret are unofficially referred to as "Feathers and Dots" and this is something Miles also wants to tell his mother. He is certain that his mom will laugh at this culturally insensitive description of both kinds of Indians and she will then be embarrassed by her own laughter.

"Miles, Miles."

He can hear his mother through the computer, but he cannot see her.

"Hey, Mom."

"I can't find the video."

"You will," he says, grinning.

Iris Murphy always has a hard time finding the video.

The fact that his mother is unaware of Margaret leaves Miles feeling slightly out-of-order and ill at ease. He has held back the information for reasons he cannot explain to himself. There is very little that Miles does not tell his mom. It is the nature of their relationship to tell. His mother has always told him information, when it was time for him to know it. She made sure that he was well prepared for school and was factually informed on the topics of sex, religion, and politics. When he asked questions about his father, his mom answered them honestly, if somewhat succinctly. Miles remembers noticing the dads in nursery school and signing to her as she put him to bed,

"Why don't I have a Dad?"

"You do have a Dad," she responded to him in sign language before pulling up his covers.

"Where is he?"

"Your dad's in Shakopee, Minnesota," she signed, spelling out "SHAKOPEE" to him.

"What does he do?"

"Your dad practices law."

"Is he a public defender like you?"

"No, he's an Indian lawyer."

"Why doesn't he live with us?"

"Your dad is married to someone else and he lives with his wife and his daughters."

"Oh."

And that was enough information for Miles then. Most of the four-year-olds at his nursery school probably thought that his grandmother picked him up because both of his parents worked. Small children understand these kinds of arrangements. Grandparents and nannies often pick up and drop off at preschools. So none of these classmates ever asked Miles about his dad.

His mom finds the video and she appears across the screen of his computer in a study off of the kitchen where she keeps her computer.

"Hey, Mom," he says, glad to see her.

"Oh, Miles, there you are," she says, smiling and waving to him. "Aren't computers a miracle?"

Growing up, Miles was adored by his mom, doted on by his nana Honora, and worshiped by his grandpa Jack. His best friend is his cousin Ezra who lives in Cincinnati. When they were boys Ezra visited every summer to Omaha with his mom and dad, Aunt Bridget and Uncle Walter, and then Miles would go home with them to Cincinnati. (Although Aunt Bridget is profoundly deaf she has always seemed much louder than his mom. Aunt Bridget has opinions on almost everything, like Grandpa Jack did. His aunt's hands seem to be in constant movement.) Two weeks later Miles would fly back to Omaha under the guard of very pretty TWA flight attendants who smelled of perfume and cigarettes. Miles knows that he enjoyed a happy and protected childhood. He is not a man with anxiety. Murphy's Law has never seemed to apply to him.

"What's going on in Omaha, Mom? How's everything?"

"Well, there's some news, sweetie," she says, pausing.

Once it was confirmed that he had a father like everyone else Miles didn't think too much about his dad the Indian lawyer in Shakopee, Minnesota. However on the first day of kindergarten at Dundee Elementary the dads came with the moms. The dads brought video cameras and the moms cried and some of the kids walking into the kindergarten classroom in straight lines cried as well. While Miles learned where to hang up his backpack and to find his nametag and to listen to his teacher, Ms. Gentilly, he thought about his dad and wondered why he wasn't there. That night as his mom reached for her eyeglasses to read to him before he fell asleep, Miles asked,

"What's his name?"

He said the words aloud rather than signing them.

"Whose name?" she asked him, looking up from her copy of **Stuart Little***, answering his words with sounds rather than signs.*

"My dad's name."

"Your dad's name is Cameron Kills Pretty Enemy."

"What kind of name is that?"

"Your dad is an enrolled member of the Standing Rock Sioux Tribe."

"What does that mean?"

"Well, that means your dad is a Native American."

"What's that?"

His mom looked down at the cover of **Stuart Little***. Her index finger*

traced the outline of the brave little mouse in his canoe.

"Your dad's an Indian."

"Like with the cowboys?"

"Yes."

"Why didn't he come to kindergarten today?"

"Your dad knew about your first day of kindergarten. I let him know how you are Miles. I send him pictures."

"Do you have a picture of him?"

"I have a photograph of him."

"Will you show me?"

"Yes, but not tonight. Let's get on with Stuart," she said, holding up the book and beginning to read.

"What's the news, Mom?"

"Well, I drove to Lincoln to see a prisoner at the penitentiary."

"Why? You hate that prison. Don't all the felons know that? Why would you go?"

"A prisoner, who I did not represent and who would not know how discomforting the state prison is for me, requested that I visit him."

"But Mom, that's crazy. You go to court. You don't go to prison. You should have that embroidered on a sofa pillow."

"Well, I filled out the papers and I visited him, despite my trepidations about bars and razor wire."

Then his mom looks away from her computer's camera.

The conversation about his dad was one of the longest ones he had ever had with his mother without using his hands. He recognized the seriousness of it all in how the words sounded. Miles remembers how willing he was that evening to give up talking about his father to listen to his mother's soothing voice as she read Stuart Little's adventures to him. Even at the age of five, Miles knew, somehow, to proceed with caution when it came to the topic of Cameron Kills Pretty Enemy.

The next day Iris Murphy showed her son a color Polaroid snapshot of a tall man in a navy blue suit, white shirt, and maroon tie. The man's arm was around his pretty young mother's waist. His mom was wearing a suit with shoulder pads and her hair was long and dark. The man's hair was also long and dark, but it was presented in two thick braids that draped on either side of the suit's lapels. Both his mom and the man were laughing as the photograph was taken in front of what Miles would learn was the University of Nebraska College of Law. On the bottom white border of the photo was the faint blue ink of an inscription in his mother's handwriting. She had written the date "1974" and the words "Cameron & Iris."

Soon after seeing his father's image Miles Murphy dreamed of Indians. The only Indians that he had ever seen were standing outside of the Public Defender's office where his mom worked, and on the walls of the Joslyn Art Museum. The Indians standing outside of the Public Defender's office wore blue jeans, military jackets, and aviator sunglasses. They smoked cigarettes. They were men and their hair was often long and black and they said, "Hey, kid," to him as he and Nana Honora walked by them on the sidewalk. Both Miles and Nana Honora said, "Hello," politely, but kept moving. Miles cannot remember how he knew that they were Indians, some adult must have told him so, but he did know that they were Indians. Later he learned to call them Native Americans.

The Indians in the paintings and photographs in the Joslyn Art Museum rode across canvases on horses, holding spears aimed at buffalo. They looked both fierce and brave with their long hair whipping in the wind of the chase. When Miles looked at these paintings he often felt sad, even before he knew he was the son of Cameron Kills Pretty Enemy. The docents that led his children's art class tours would always give a brief history of the land that was the Louisiana Purchase before settlers and pioneers made their way across it by Conestoga wagon or on foot to the Great Plains of Nebraska and beyond. The voices of the docents sounded wistful as they described the documentary quality of the portraits of Karl Bodmer and of a world now gone. Even in preschool summer camps, where things like war, genocide, and the politics of colonial countries were skirted carefully, Miles understood that this vivid way of life was "extinct" and as faraway as "ancient history," something that Nana Honora spoke of when she talked of Ireland, where *the Murphys and the O'Donnells were once kings and queens as real as President Jack Kennedy.*

In Miles's dream, thousands of Indians on painted ponies wearing eagle feather headdresses and full war paint rode their horses from the Council Bluffs in Iowa on the eastern side of the Missouri River into Omaha. He stood alone on the corner of 50th and Dodge Streets, watching as the Indians made their way past the Pittman Animal Hospital, Merle Norman Cosmetics, the Dundee Dell, and the Dundee Theatre. The horses kicked up the litter and the leaves from the street's gutters and the men chanted songs in a language Miles did not then know, but he knew that they were there to take Omaha back to some time that was long before Miles ever lived. Afraid, but stuck in his dream, he stood his ground on the thin slice of sidewalk that bordered Dodge Street. In the middle of the riders rode Cameron Kills Pretty Enemy. His dad was dressed in the same blue suit and maroon tie of the snapshot, and Miles called out to him,

"Hey, Dad, it's me, Miles."

Over the years Miles has dreamt this dream many times, but Cameron Kills Pretty Enemy never replies to him. He knows the dream is also the reality of his relationship with his father. Cameron Kills Pretty Enemy appears, he never calls, and rarely does he respond to any form of communication from his son.

Miles was in second grade when he first saw his dad who was sitting on the front steps of the Murphy house on Cass Street. It was April. The trees were in bloom and the air smelled of flowers that Miles could not name. Nana Honora was walking with Miles home from school.

"Hello Cameron," his nana said.

"Hello Mrs. Murphy," the man on the steps replied, "I'm here to see my boy."

"We should call Iris," his grandmother said.

"No need to do that," he said, standing up to a height that was much taller than both Miles and his grandmother.

"I'll call Jack then."

Cameron Kills Pretty Enemy winced.

"You know that Jack is not going to want to see me, Mrs. Murphy."

"That certainly is the truth, Cameron," she said, walking past him up the steps to unlock the front door, leaving Miles alone with his father.

"Hello Miles."

"Hello," Miles said to the man in the blue Polo golf shirt, blue jeans, and cowboy boots, and his hair in one very long braid.

"Do you know who I am?"

"You're my dad."

"Cameron Kills Pretty Enemy," he said, sticking his hand out to Miles. "I just happened to be in town and thought that I might meet you."

Miles shook his father's hand firmly as his grandfather had taught him to do.

"Would you like to come in? I'll get you a glass of milk and some graham crackers."

His dad nodded and followed him into the house.

Under his nana's protective gaze, Miles shared his after school snack with his father at the kitchen table. They did not talk. When Cameron Kills Pretty Enemy finished his snack, he stood up, taking his glass and plate to the kitchen sink. With a wave and a wink he slipped out the back door moments before Iris Murphy and her father arrived to confront him. His mother was hard pressed to hide the look of disappointment that crossed her face when she saw Miles alone at the table. His grandfather's angry demeanor turned to relief and he turned on heel to drive back to the fire station.

Cameron Kills Pretty Enemy's parenting could be defined by the random nature of his presence in the life of his son. Once he came to Miles' eighth grade soccer tournament, standing alone on the edge of the field isolated from all of the other parents, speaking to no one, not even to Miles. His dad came to every one of Miles's parent- teacher conferences at Creighton Prep, sitting beside, Iris, Jack and Honora Murphy in classroom after classroom. These visits elicited the frequent comment from his grandfather,

"That Cameron scares the Jesuits. They don't know what to make of the giant Indian with all the questions about algorithms and Thomas Aquinas."

What Miles noted, without mentioning it to his mom, was that everyone got a glimpse of Cameron Kills Pretty Enemy when Miles was in high school, but Miles. When Miles moved to Lincoln, Cameron began to show up at his dormitory on the campus of the University of Nebraska, sitting silently in the lobby of Schramm Hall until Miles returned from classes. Inevitably they would eat dinner at Valentino's Pizza.

"How's your mom?" Cameron would ask him.

"Mom's fine."

"She's a very smart lady."

"How's your wife?" Miles learned to ask.

"Elizabeth Anne is well," Cameron would say, often adding, "She's very busy with her money."

His father's wife, Elizabeth Anne Kills Pretty Enemy nee White Crow, is an enrolled member of the Shakopee Mdewakanton Sioux Tribe in Shakopee, Minnesota. Her tribe runs the Mystic Lake Casino in Prior Lake, an extraordinarily successful endeavor. Cameron and Elizabeth Anne have three daughters — Willow, Lily, and Eunice — who are active in the tribe and have a food and decorating show on HGTV called "Native Places/Native Spaces."

"I need to see you, Miles, to hear myself think," his dad always said to him during those dinners in Lincoln, and later when he visited Nagoya when Miles was studying at Nanzan University. Cameron appeared unannounced in Dakar during Miles' Peace Corps assignment in Senegal. His dad has turned up at every embassy where Miles has served, including, Islamabad, since his acceptance into the Foreign Service. With little fanfare Cameron presents himself at the checkpoint outside an embassy, offering the security officer both his passport with visas and his tribal enrollment card. Embassy staffers are startled at the tall Indian whose braids are now silver, but Miles is not.

"My daughters chirp like a flock of sparrows. They chatter like birds. Talk is endless in my house," Cameron has told him on every visit. *"When the birds are too loud in the morning I know that I need to see you, Miles. I know that my son will give me peace and quiet."*

The unpredictability of his father's visits keeps Miles longing for them. Cameron Kills Pretty Enemy has yet to travel to Nairobi, but Miles knows that when he least expects it, Cameron will appear. It is his way. Cameron will eat whatever Miles offers him, sharing with his son the happenings of life in Shakopee and sometimes the politics in South Dakota. He will sleep on a pallet on the floor of Miles's apartment, refusing his son's bed. There will be a few days of sightseeing and then Miles will wake up one morning to a stillness in his apartment and know before getting out of bed that his father is gone. After his father's visits his colleagues look at him differently, as do the people in the small restaurants where Miles takes his meals. American Indians, those other kinds of Indians, are a rare sight, even in most of the United States. People outside of the United States sense the uniqueness of the moment when their eyes fall on Cameron Kills Pretty Enemy; they are glad to shake his hand on introduction.

"Your father's like the real deal, isn't he?" a friend in Islamabad said to Miles. "He's fearless coming to Pakistan, brave."

Miles nodded.

"So you're an Indian, too?"

"I'm part Indian, but I'm not enrolled in a tribe."

"Why not?"

"It's sort like a country club and I haven't quite got the sponsorship."

"But Miles, you've got the looks."

Miles laughed, ending the conversation.

Iris Murphy communicates with her son, weekly, and sometimes daily, but she has never traveled abroad to visit him. Miles has noticed that his mother seems to go no further than Minneapolis or Chicago in her sojourns since the deaths of his grandparents. Her curiosity about her son's assignments seems insatiable and she peppers their talks on Skype with questions about Nairobi and African politics and the legal system. She reads *The New York Times* and *The Economist* online and gleans both information and her queries from them.

Iris is the lodestone that brings Miles back home to Omaha and the comfort of their house on Cass Street. His godfather, Paul Simmons, told him once that his mom lives for his returns to Nebraska. Miles understands his godfather to be as dramatic as his father is understated. Each of them presents a kind of partial truth that Miles knows needs to be considered about what manhood actually is. Of course, Paul and Cameron have been not-so-friendly rivals since their University of Nebraska Law School days. Both were enamored of Iris Murphy and both made Law Review. This is something his Nana Honora told him.

"Why did this guy in Lincoln want to see you, Mom?"

The whole concept of prison disturbs his mother. Miles knows that she despises mandatory sentencing. The expression "war on drugs" can make her laugh bitterly.

"The prisoner is someone I knew growing up."

"Is he somebody, I know, Mom?"

"No, he's somebody that Aunt Bridget knows. I dated him in high school."

Miles has no interest in any of his mom's former boyfriends. He considers them to be assholes because most of them have made her sad. His mother, he believes, is far too romantic and way too softhearted. Marriage is about realism and direct conversation. Iris Murphy thinks it's about falling in love. It is good that his mom has never married for as wise as she is about the law she is a fool for love.

"Why is he in prison?"

"He was stopped on a suspected DUI and he put his car into reverse and knocked down the police officer who was approaching the car. The officer was badly hurt."

"Did he help the cop?"

"No, he sped away, leaving him on the side of the road."

"Why would you visit a guy like that, Mom? He's a jerk."

"I visited him because he sent me a request. I thought he might need my help. He's profoundly deaf, Miles."

Miles feels guilty when his mother tells him this. He thinks of his aunt Bridget and all that his grandparents did to make sure that she had an education. They learned American Sign Language and then sent her to boarding school in Cincinnati.

"Did you help him?"

"No, I didn't."

His mother pauses and he stares into the computer screen at her. She is dressed in a gray and black sweater and black leggings, her at home wear. Her silver hair is pulled back away from her face. She has applied a bold color of lipstick. In her hands is a scarlet colored mug from which she sips a milky colored coffee. For a time she is quiet.

Silence is the quality that defines his encounters with Cameron Kills

Pretty Enemy while the noise of communication, whether in American Sign Language or speech, is the hallmark of his upbringing in the Murphy household. It still astounds Miles that his tiny, beautifully dressed, dependable Mom was attracted to this giant, mostly silent, seemingly nomadic man. When he was a student at the University of Nebraska Miles once asked her,

"What did the two of you ever talk about?"

"We didn't so much talk as argue."

"What did you argue about?"

"Law, ethics, history."

"How could you argue and like him at the same time?"

"Well, argument is Cameron's pretext for conversation. I don't think he knows how to make small talk. It is all big talk or no talk with him."

"Did you love him?"

"Yes."

"Did he love you?"

"I hope so."

"How did I happen then?"

"I hadn't see Cameron for years. He was a married man in law school, so no matter how I felt about him, I didn't express it."

"So ..."

"One day I walked out of the Douglas County Courthouse and there he was standing at the bottom of the steps, looking up at me. It was autumn and I was in flux and had been attracted to Cameron for years. We went straight to my apartment from the courthouse. You were conceived that evening. He left in the middle of the night. I did not hear him leave. Three months later he sent me a letter, explaining that he loved me, but he loved Elizabeth Anne, too, and that he could not see me again. He wanted to raise his daughters," and his mom paused, looking away from him, but not tearing up. Then she added, *"Cameron did not say he was sorry. Cameron is never sorry."*

"Mom, that's horrible."

"I have you and you're what I really wanted."

"Why would he do that?"

"At the time I don't think your dad ever considered that what we were doing could make a baby."

Miles knows that a cloud shadowed his birth and that the Murphy family is not a fan of drama, particularly the bickering fights about nothing that dominate the daily lives of so many people. They were talkers, but not the kind of talkers that would ever be on reality television.

"Oh, it's a soap opera," Nana Honora used to say when she really didn't want to go into a subject. "They made a hash of it."

The soap opera of Cameron Kills Pretty Enemy's legal work Miles has learned about in serious and anonymous bursts of words such as "the restraining order" or "when she went to rehab" or "they lost the baby." These slivers of description would hang in the air between bites of pizza or falafel. Once or twice Miles has posed a question or two after hearing these declarations, but his dad is not a man to take questions.

Lost in her thoughts, his mother does not speak, nor does she move her hands.

Finally he asks her,

"Then why did this guy request to see you?"

She looks up and directly at him.

"It appears that someone at the prison has it out for me."

"Shit, Mom."

"Language, Miles."

"But, Mom," he says, but she stops him by raising her hand.

"A felon named Angelo Bartlett does not like me. He has been telling people at the prison that he is going to get even with me, you know, do things to the house."

"What kind of felon is he?"

"Angelo Bartlett is a pimp and purveyor of child pornography and he probably has tax issues as well. They all do."

"Do you know him? Did you ever represent him?"

"No. Pimps have enough money to hire attorneys. I may have represented one of the girls who worked for him, but I can't recall anyone connected to Angelo Bartlett. Sometimes people just take a dislike to an individual. It is irrational, and it happens a lot."

Through the screen of the computer his mother looks small, like a mouse in her dusky colors, and defenseless.

Miles would like to yell at her. She lives alone and everyone in Omaha knows where she lives. Large yard signs scream out her minority political affiliations and she is always working in the garden. None of this bothered him when his grandparents were alive, but now it is a constant underlying worry for him. It isn't like she works in the backroom of a flower shop.

"Have you called the police?"

"Yes."

"Has this Angelo Bartlett done anything?"

She looks away before speaking.

"Someone through a baseball threw the window of the storm door on the back of the house. They left a mound of dog poop outside that door."

"Then you need to get out of the house for awhile, Mom. Go stay with Martha or Uncle Paul."

"I was thinking about getting a dog, Miles. Your cousin Ezra could help me get a dog."

"Well, first Ezra will have to locate that dog. You need to get away from the house until you have a dog."

"But I need to protect the property."

"No, Mom, you need to sell the property."

"But, Miles, you grew up here. This is our home."

"I'm not kidding. You're young and you can start a whole new life in a condo with security where no one will know where you live. The house is a burden for one person and this crap just shows what a burden it is."

His mother seems to recede from him on the computer screen as he says these words. She sighs, looks over her shoulder towards the kitchen, and then says,

"The police are working on it. What's new in Nairobi?"

For a moment, Miles cannot speak. He hates this kind of passive aggressive behavior that his mother knows so well from the courtroom and negotiations. Rarely does she use it with him, but when she does it is always the same. Drop the bomb and then segue onto an entirely unrelated topic. His heart is pounding and his hands are shaking. He doesn't know what to say to her end run. So he decides to tell her his news. Even though he feels that it is too good and too happy, in light of her revelation. Without the gloss of his planned introduction, he says,

"I'm in love with a woman named Margaret D'Souza. I'm going to ask her to marry me."

Iris Murphy, his mom, turns away from her view of the kitchen. Her smile lights up the computer screen. She goes from looking like a mouse to a chipper sparrow.

"Goodness, Miles, this is wonderful. Tell me all about her. There's nothing better than love."

And with that he tells his mother everything about Margaret. They speak of weddings and diamond rings and a trip to Omaha. For twenty minutes the sun shines on their conversation. And just as things are winding down Miles remembers to ask.

"Mom, you never told me the outcome of the colonoscopy the doctor recommended."

"That was weeks ago."

"So, it was nothing?"

"Well, they found something in the colon."

"Was it a polyp?'

"Well, the gastroenterologist then said I needed another test."

"And?"

"So they did a CT scan of my liver and the area around it."

"Did they find anything, Mom?"

From her office chair in Omaha his mom sighs.

Then she signs the words to him, "I have cancer in my colon and in my liver."

Miles begins to perspire.

"What do the doctors want to do, Mom?" his hands say back to her.

"The oncologist has a plan. I'm going to begin with an oral chemo-therapy to shrink the tumors and then a surgeon will cut out what's left. He's very optimistic."

"Do you want me to come home? Don't you think I should come home?"

"Not yet."

"When?"

"Bring Margaret home this summer."

"But Mom."

"It will all be clearer then."

"I love you," he says aloud, as his fist goes to his chest, thumping it.

"It's all going to be okay, Miles. Sometimes life moves faster than we expect it will, however." She says this, dropping her hands and re-turning to her voice.

"Mom, who knows about your diagnosis?"

"Well, you and Martha and Paul and the sergeant in Property Crime at the Police Department. And Aunt Bridget and Uncle Walter."

"Not Cameron?"

"Your father doesn't respond to my calls, Miles."

"Don't worry about him, Mom. Just take care of yourself."

Then his mom smiles at him and he feels it is possible that all could be right in his world. He will call Margaret. Margaret will know what he should do. She always does. Her family is filled with doctors and scientists.

"Everything's going to be okay."

"You sound like your grandfather."

"I love you," he signs again.

And then she blows him a kiss.

"You'd better go to bed, Miles. It's late in Nairobi."

"You're always in my prayers, Mom."

"And you in mine, sweetie."

For a moment they look at each other in the wonder of a mother and child.

Grift Bred in the Bone

Emily Morton sits behind the steering wheel of her ancient Mercedes Benz, a car the color of goldenrod. The oldest boy sits next to her in the passenger seat. In the back seat his brothers are squeezed in on either side of the cage for Emily's parrot Herman. Herman is an Amazon green and he is older than all three of these boys put together. The parrot, Emily believes, is the reincarnation of Elvis Presley and he loves her like a husband, or at least, better than any husband Emily has had. The three boys, even the eight-year-old, will soon be out of her universe. She has felt it in her bones for the past week and yesterday it was confirmed. Her daughter, Stephanie, is marrying the Mormon.

"Look, Mom, you need to bring the boys home now," Stephanie said to her on the cell phone, after the boys had fallen asleep in the vacation-rental-by-owner apartment that Emily booked for two weeks in Omaha.

There was a pause after this pronouncement as Stephanie inhaled. Over thirteen hundred miles separate Omaha from Las Vegas but Emily could still smell the smoke of her daughter's Marlboro Light. It filled the studio apartment. The smoke floated over the towheads of the three boys who slept sprawled out across the floor on pallets made of quilts and Mexican blankets.

"Mormons don't smoke, Stephanie."

"Frank is buying me an electronic cigarette."

"Oh."

"So I told Frank that you and the boys are on a buying trip for Uncle Ron's club and that you are homeschooling them along the way. Mormons like homeschoolers."

"Ron hasn't spoken to me in years."

"Be that as it may, Mom, that's what Frank thinks, and you and the boys need to come home for the wedding."

"But I need the boys for Saint Louis and Memphis. We were going to do open houses in Clayton and Germantown."

"Stephanie, Stephanie," Herman intoned from his perch on Emily's shoulder.

"The boys can't do Clayton or Germantown, because they will be moving into our new house in Henderson."

"But I need them."

"No, I need them, Mom. And you need to send me my cut of their work money now."

"I said that I would pay you after the trip."

"I had to quit the club, Mom."

"Why?"

"Because good Mormons are not in topless dance reviews."

"Well, your Mormon sure liked visiting that club when you were in that review."

"I need to pay the rent."

"Won't he pay it?"

"Frank won't pay for anything until we are married and we won't be having sex until we are married now that I've converted. So Frank wants to get married pronto. He's getting no milk from this cow until there's a wedding band around my ring finger and my name on his checking account."

"The boys are angels. They're naturals. Everyone loves them."

"Everyone loves them," Herman echoed Emily.

"I expect all of you home by next Saturday and a money order to-morrow."

"But…"

"Mom, I can call your probation officer."

"We'll be home by Sunday."

"Bitch," Herman intoned.

"Saturday, and tell Herman to shut up."

Elliott, Carter, and Spencer Westby are dressed in khakis, Madras shirts, boy-sized blue sport coats, and Sperry topsiders. They are All-American boys at the ages of 10, 8, and 6-years. As Emily walks through the open houses of the Dundee and Fairacres neighborhoods the three boys talk to the realtors, charming them. Emily has coached them in the enchanting arts. Someday they will slay the hearts of the girls that come their way. In most cases there is nothing to be found in these houses, because the realtors tell the owners to put everything of value in safe deposit boxes. Stressed out owners do slip up and forget things, however, and this is the point of these tours for Emily. She finds three hundred dollars in the sock drawer of the bureau in the master bedroom of a house on Happy Hollow Boulevard. And she discovers a small vial of cocaine hidden in an ice bucket in the media room of a house on North Elmwood Road and a pair of diamond stud earrings in a bottle of Viagra in a bathroom cabinet as well. She will sell the drugs to a gentleman dealer she knows in Kansas City on the trip home. When they hit Denver she will start wearing the earrings.

The boys have no idea what Emily Morton does for their living. The aura of their innocence propels the trust that people put in their gracious grandmother. Trust is at the heart of a grift, but all that Emily is doing, really, is stealing, something at which she is accomplished. There is no theft by swindle involved in her daily routine with these boys. On the days when there are no open houses in the cities that they visit Emily takes the boys to public libraries. There they study their homeschooling textbooks and she checks her EBay accounts. Later they stop by a United Parcel Service where she mails packages to her customers. The boys never notice the small items that Emily slips into her purse when they are perusing antique stores and upscale houses for sale. Nor do they know about the credit cards and drivers licenses that she has lifted out of handbags in Whole Foods stores across the Rocky Mountain West. Emily uses these cards and licenses discreetly, and only once. She buys reasonable things — food, gas, lodging — before cutting them up and tossing them into dumpsters. In her mind they are necessities and what she does is her job. This is not the view of her Reno based parole officer, Vincent Lawrence, but so be it. It is the truth as Emily sees it.

It helps that Emily Morton is elegant and beautiful, and of a certain age. Her Mercedes is classic and in great mechanical condition thanks to a young Austrian mechanic in Reno and the dry air of Nevada. It would be even more helpful if she could teach her grandsons the tricks of a grifter, as Emily's mother taught her. Then she could do far more business. But she promised Stephanie that she wouldn't.

"If these boys learn anything, Mom, I will call Vincent in a heartbeat. No sticky finger tricks, no noisy neighborhood diversions as you send them into pilfer the houses of America's most wealthy."

"I would never …"

"Don't even start with me about what 'you would never.'"

Emily could feel her gromace through the cell towers of the Rocky ountain West.

"I promise."

"You're too old for prison, Mom."

Emily does not have the moxie left in her to return to any kind of confinement. She just wants to earn a little money before settling into a studio apartment near Stephanie and the kids. After the open houses and then lunch, she and the boys will leave Omaha. She has promised them

French fries, hamburgers, and Cokes at a restaurant called the Dundee Dell on Dodge Street. (Stephanie is a strict vegan and the boys adhere to her diet when they are at home. Emily has introduced them to all kinds of meat and cheese on their travels. The boys move between the worlds of meat and tofu seamlessly. They are children of Las Vegas. What happens outside of Nevada is never discussed.) She parks the Mercedes on a quiet part of California Street underneath an oak tree, rolling each window down two inches for Herman. The parrot is disturbed by the noise of busy streets and he hates parking lots. The boys understand the bird's anxieties and are used to making these walks.

When they arrive at the Dundee Dell the three boys charm the young woman who is serving them with their unprompted "please" and then "thank you" and she takes their orders with a smile. They place paper napkins in their laps and eat buns, burgers, and fries in an intense silence. Emily has trained them never to tell their names or say anything when eating in public. When the server returns to see their empty plates, she announces,

"You boys have earned ice cream on the house."

"Thank you," they say in a chorus.

Emily nods her head, smiles, and hands her a recently stolen credit card. It is accepted. She signs the receipt with the name that is on the stolen card and leaves the server seven dollars as a tip.

Elliott and Carter use the restroom before leaving the restaurant, but not Spencer. Emily knows that before they hit Council Bluffs Spencer will want to take a leak on the side of the Interstate, but she never chides her grandchildren. That is what Stephanie their now Mormon, formerly Seventh Day Adventist, mother is for back in Las Vegas. Also correcting children in public draws attention. What Emily creates with her grandsons is an image of good looks and excellent behavior. The boys look like a snapshot from of *Town & Country*. They could be the poster children for a country club or private boarding school. "Why can't you be like them?" women will ask their unruly offspring, when looking at the Westby boys in a McDonald's.

As the four of them walk to the car, Spencer runs ahead and begins a conversation with a white-haired woman who is working in her garden. The yard is enclosed within a wrought iron fence. Spencer is at the gate. Emily can see a large dog walk up to the side of the woman.

"That's my grandmother," she hears Spencer tell the woman.

"Well, I will ask her then," the woman says.

"Is it okay, if your grandson uses my restroom?" the woman calls down the street to Emily. "It seems he has to go."

Elliott and Carter snicker. Emily looks at them, raising one eyebrow. The boys compose their faces to blandness. "That is very kind of you," she says.

"He says that you're on your way out of town."

"Yes, that is the case," Emily tells her when she reaches the gate where Spencer is standing. The boy has the look of a child on the verge of an accident. "I'm sorry," she says to the white-haired woman. "He said he didn't have to go at the restaurant."

"Don't worry, I have a powder room just inside my front door," she says, grasping the dog by his collar and then opening the gate.

The dog snarls at Spencer. Spencer freezes. His eyes open wide.

"Sit, Ferragamo." the woman says, her free hand raised.

Emily and her grandsons don't move. They watch as the white-haired woman wraps two small hands around the animal's thick leather collar. The dog sits. The woman pauses, saying nothing. The dog waits, as do the people. Everything is still. Finally, the woman walks the dog across the yard to a lead that she has staked underneath a walnut tree and attaches the lead to the collar.

"Stay," she says, again offering the dog a hand signal.

The dog whimpers and then lies down next to a large Obama-Biden 2012 sign, as the woman returns to the garden gate, offering Spencer her hand.

Spencer takes her hand. He is small for his six-years. She smiles and Spencer says, "Thank you."

They walk down the path to the front door and Emily, Elliott, Carter, and the dog wait in silence. They are on a schedule. The woman comes out the door and walks back to them.

"Do you two need the bathroom?"

"No, thank you," says Elliott.

"No, thank you," says Carter.

"My Miles always said he didn't have to go and then he always had to go once we were a twenty-five miles from home and cornfields all around."

"Yes," Emily says. "I know."

The two boys nod their heads. Spencer does not come. Another dog in the neighborhood barks. Ferragamo looks up, but he does not bark in response. His eyes are on the people in his yard. He turns his head to look at the door.

"Do you boys have a dog?"

"No, we don't," Elliott tells her.

"But Grandmother says we might get one this summer," Carter adds. "Grandmother says that boys should have dogs."

Emily smiles and the woman smiles at her.

"My father was a firefighter and he loved dogs. So he gave my son, Miles, a dog and my nephew, Ezra, one as well. Ferragamo is new to me. He is gift from Ezra."

"We want a golden retriever," says Elliott.

"And so does Grandmother," Carter says.

"I'm sure your grandmother does," the woman tells them. "Dogs can be such a comfort as companions."

Emily nods her head in the uncommitted fashion of a bobble-headed doll. She turns her eyes once again to the woman's front door, afraid for just a moment that something bad has happened to her youngest grandson. But suddenly Spencer appears, pushing the screen door open. He is grinning until he sees her face. Then he runs down the stairs and tears down the path, crying, "Thank you, thank you." The dog notices, sitting up.

"You're welcome, you're welcome," the woman says.

"Thank you so much," Emily says, as well. "I'm so sorry for the inconvenience."

"There was nothing inconvenient about it."

"We have to be going."

"They're great boys."

For a moment Emily Morton looks at her grandsons, and then back at the elegant woman before her who wears a Lily Pulitzer sundress, pink driving moccasins, and white leather gardening gloves, like something out of *The New York Times* Sunday Style section. Emily thinks that the silver-haired woman belongs in the frame of their picture with her blooming peonies in the background. For a moment, she knows that God is looking down from his heavens and thinking, *This is good.*

"Grifters believe in God," Emily's mother always told her. "Grifters have ethics, we are not common. We will not be condemned to hell. Christ forgave the thief who believed. And we believe."

"They are," she says.

Emily hears the note of gratitude in her own voice.

Elliott and Carter break into shy smiles while Spencer blushes.

"Boys, it's time to go home," Emily says and the three boys wave to the woman and the dog in the background.

As they walk down the block they can hear Herman squawking, "Hurry up, hurry up," from the Mercedes.

Emily is glad to hear the engine turn over. She is thrilled to drive east on Dodge Street to its connection to Interstate 29 South. She has a meeting scheduled in Kansas City. By the time she crosses the Missouri

River the boys are asleep. Three hours and twenty minutes later they arrive in the Country Club District of that city.

Emily parks the car on a tree-lined street of lovely homes. They will walk into the Plaza to meet her contact. It is mid-May and there is plenty of daylight left. Herman squawks, "We're here, we're here."

Elliott and Carter open the doors and get out, waiting for Emily and Spencer on the sidewalk. They stretch and talk about dogs. Indeed she has promised them a golden retriever at the end of this trip. Stephanie is allergic to dogs. Emily will have to find an apartment that will allow her a dog and the parrot.

"Grandmother," Spencer says.

"Yes, Spencer."

Emily turns to look at him over the back of her seat. He is a beautiful child, red-cheeked and sleepy-eyed. His lips are still heart-shaped like a baby's.

"Here it is," he says, pulling from a pocket in his khaki pants a bank envelope that he hands over to her. "It's for you."

"For you," Herman repeats the words, like Elvis would, like any good husband should.

Inside is six hundred dollars in fifty dollars bills. Emily's heart swells with pride. The child notices, she thinks. The grift is bred in his bones.

"We won't talk about this, Spencer," she says. "It's just between you and me."

"I know."

A shadow crosses his face.

"She was a nice lady," Spencer says. "She let me use her bathroom."

"She was, Spencer. But losing this money won't break her and it will save me."

Spencer looks out the window at his brothers. Emily can see that

Grift Bred in the Bone   127

he is thinking. She won't push the child. This will be the end of it. If Stephanie finds out she will report Emily to her probation officer, Mr. Vincent Lawrence. Emily sighs.

"I won't tell Mom."

"Thank you," Emily says.

"You're welcome," her grandson says with sincerity.

"You're welcome," the parrot echoes.

One Thesis

AT HALF PAST TEN on Wednesday morning, May 16, 2012, Erma Charging walks out of her last statistics class at Saint Olaf College in Northfield, Minnesota. Finals will begin on Friday. Erma then drives to work as an unpaid intern at Kills Pretty Enemy LLP, a law office in Prior Lake. Cameron Kills Pretty Enemy is her father's second cousin and a member of her father's congregation at St. Timothy's Lutheran Church in Lakeville. Pastor Paul Charging and his cousin are both enrolled members of the Standing Rock Sioux Tribe, as are Erma and her brother Peter.

Erma's mother, Nadine, is from Jamaica, the country, not the neighborhood in the New York City borough of Queens. Nadine Johns Charging was raised as an Anglican in Kingston, but converted to the Evangelical Lutheran Church of America, after meeting Paul Charging at a cricket match in Bryn Mawr Park in Minneapolis. Erma's mother is passionate about cricket and Paul Charging learned to play the sport to impress his future wife. It did.

Like many Jamaicans, Nadine is a devout Christian. She converted to her husband's church, after "great introspection," and then her conversion was "whole- hearted." These particular phrases in her parents' courtship story never change, no matter how many times Erma asks her mother to tell it. Nadine sings in the choir at St. Timothy's and after services she is a focal point in the vestibule, smiling and hugging people. Mrs. Charging wears brightly colored clothing every Sunday, and under her white coat at the Target in Savage, where she works as a pharmacist.

Erma understands that her mother stands out, but she also realizes that if Nadine wore gray and brown and never said a word she would be noticed as well. To be a handful of brown people among a large group of people who consider themselves to be white, but are really rather pink to beige, is to be distinct and that has always been the situation for the Charging family in Lakeville. An influx of Somali and Mexican immigrants has expanded the complexion of the community, but that is a recent development.

"The Charging family," as Pastor Paul says, "has been here to welcome the strangers in our midst and give them haven for many years."

To be passionately fearless about being who one is, and to be that person with joy, could be the definition of a Jamaican. Erma knows that it is the definition of Nadine. In personality, Erma resembles her grandmother Clarice Charging, a sweet and reserved woman who lives in McLaughlin, South Dakota on the Standing Rock Reservation. Grandma Clarice is retired from the Fort Yates Hospital where she worked as a licensed practical nurse. Like her grandmother, Erma freezes in the spotlight. Both women use words sparingly, but when they speak their words are important.

Dorothy Archambault who attends St. Timothy's and works for Cameron Kills Pretty Enemy, as both his paralegal and office administrator, noticed Erma's quiet and extremely orderly ways. Dorothy offered her a highly sought after, yet unpaid Wednesday internship when she learned that Erma had created the St. Timothy's website. It is stellar. Erma is also majoring in mathematics and she is quite handy with Excel spreadsheet calculations.

"I cannot keep up with the website and the statistics that Mr. Kills Pretty Enemy needs. Most of the interns are not interested in that part of our work. They want to carry Mr. Kills Pretty Enemy's bags into court, or go with him when he lobbies in Saint Paul. You would be perfect, Erma. You can actually do something for us."

Erma has worked quietly and diligently since nursery school.

"Well, I think I can do it," Erma said, pausing. "I have only one class on Wednesday and that is early in the morning."

"Great," Dorothy Archambault said. "Then it's settled."

"But …"

"There's a but?"

"Eventually I want to be paid."

Dorothy looked shocked. "You want to be paid?"

"Yes."

"But all we offer are unpaid internships. They provide a wealth of experience and connections. Mr. Kills Pretty Enemy advises political and business leaders. He settles tribal disputes. You should be honored that I have made you this offer."

"But it is work, Mrs. Archambault. I will be working for Cameron …"

Dorothy raises her hand, stopping Erma's words.

"You mean Mr. Kills Pretty Enemy."

"Mr. Kills Pretty Enemy."

"We shall see," Dorothy said, raising an eyebrow.

Erma is not a fool. She wrote a gracious note to Dorothy Archambault accepting the internship and thanking her for it. Many college students would kill for the opportunity that Dorothy offered her, but Erma still recoils at the notion of unpaid internships in for-profit-environments. If her cousin Cameron is for anything he is for profit, but that is a family reality and not something Erma would ever share with Dorothy. No family member would seek Cameron's counsel without a checkbook nearby. His pro bono work will never include shirttail cousins with shady backgrounds.

"One must pay for one's sins," is a well-known Cameron aphorism.

Most Wednesdays Dorothy is in the office. It is Dorothy who answers the telephone. Dorothy takes messages and assures the caller that "Mr. Kills Pretty Enemy will be in touch with you by the end of the day." Cameron will return the calls of all of these potential clients during the supper hour, because as Dorothy says, "That is a good time to reach people."

Erma's cousin is in the office, but he is only available by telephone to "Kurt BlueDog, William Hardacker, the office of the Governor of Minnesota, the office of the President of the United States, or the Attorney General of the United States."

Dorothy made Erma recite this list three times on the day of her training.

"And remember to take messages from the Office of the Attorney General of Minnesota. We would never put that call through to Mr. Kills Pretty Enemy on a Wednesday."

Puzzled and curious, Erma asked, "Why not?"

"If you live in Minnesota long enough, Erma, you will come to learn that 'A.G.' stands for 'Almost Governor' and Mr. Kills Pretty Enemy does not take phone calls from an 'Almost Governor' on Wednesdays."

"Yes, Mrs. Archambault."

Twenty minutes later Erma put forth another question. The query came from her many years of babysitting. It popped out of her quite developed frontal lobe and across her lips instinctually. For Erma, it was an important interrogatory because it involved family.

"What if Mr. Kills Pretty Enemy's wife calls? Or one of his daughters? What if it's an emergency? Wouldn't we have him pick up the phone?"

"There are no emergencies in the Kills Pretty Enemy household on Wednesdays. His family knows this. They will be well. They will carry on. They will not call."

As the daughter of a pastor, Erma knows that emergencies always happen and they always happen in the middle of the night or when the Charging family is on a vacation to McLaughlin or Kingston. People reach Paul Charging and he always takes the calls. The pastor is always available. But she does not question her supervisor's statement, for that is what Dorothy is, her supervisor.

"If you need a recommendation, or need to list a supervisor on an application you should use my name, because I am your supervisor and I will write your letters of recommendation, not Mr. Kills Pretty Enemy."

"Yes, Mrs. Archambault."

Erma thinks of Mrs. Archambault as "Dorothy" just as she thinks of Mr. Kills Pretty Enemy as "Cameron," but part of her unpaid work is to follow the rules that she has been given so she always refers to them as she has been instructed. If Dorothy chattered and interrupted Erma's work then Erma knows she would grow to dislike the rules. This dislike would cloud her drive to Prior Lake and remind her that she was not being paid for her considerable work. But Dorothy works very hard and Erma is comfortable in an atmosphere of silence and in that way Erma and Dorothy are made for each other. They prefer quiet. And each woman, young and old, is very good at the most important rule of Kills Pretty Enemy LLP, their clients' right to privacy.

Every Wednesday when Dorothy answers the phone she takes calls from names that Erma knows. Many are for legal representation for driving while under the influence and others are for drug offenses and assault. Others seek recommendations for counsel in regards to divorce. They are family names from the church and her high school. The stories that Dorothy so carefully inscribes onto a yellow legal pad in her neat longhand are all sad. Dorothy knows what questions to ask.

"Is the boy in the Hennepin County Juvenile Detention Center?" or

"Was there a weapon involved?"

Dorothy knows what to do.

"I am calling 911," and she does so on her smart phone. Notes taken, tragedy averted, she returns to the screen of her computer, not saying a word to the intern sitting at the next desk about the drama she has just averted.

Erma has come to very much admire her supervisor and to be sweetly puzzled by her cousin. What Cameron does all day on Wednesdays is listen to classical music on Minnesota Public Radio and read books, often crime fiction, and works of history. He wears soft brown moccasins and sips peppermint tea while eating the thin mint cookies sold by local Girl Scouts every spring. Most of the day he spends stretched out on the leather couch that is across from the picture window in his office, resting his bad knees. A star quilt covers his considerable frame and his reading glasses are halfway down the bridge of his nose. Cameron's long white hair falls loosely around his shoulders on his day off. He looks like a grandfather when he falls asleep with a novel on his chest. When he sleeps he snores. The door to his office is always open. Cameron can hear the calls that Dorothy takes, but he never says a word. Erma can feel him listening and refraining from jumping into the fray.

And only on Wednesdays does he have the photographs out on the credenza behind his expansive desk. They are a chronology of a boy from infancy to manhood. A dark-haired, white woman holds the infant that morphs into a toddler, schoolboy, college student, and, finally, a smiling man with his arm around Cameron. The photographs are never out on the days when Dorothy and Cameron call their sporadic, but required intern meetings. The mixed race boy looks like Cameron Kills Pretty Enemy, but he certainly is not the spitting image of him. Erma's heart beats faster when she glances through the doorway at the photographs. The man with his arm around Cameron is handsome. He is, Erma's private crush, her George Clooney. This is her secret. Cameron's office is full of secrets on Wednesdays.

On this particular Wednesday in the middle of May, Erma is alone in the reception area. Dorothy had a medical appointment after lunch and will not be returning to the office until Thursday. The phone has not been ringing, but if it does it will go to the answering machine. It is a good day for Dorothy to be away.

After updating the Kills Pretty Enemy LLP website calendars Erma adds a vast amount of figures to the Excel spreadsheets that Cameron keeps on reservation crimes across North America. She sighs. These numbers make her very sad. It is 4:00 p.m. and she will leave in an hour. Erma turns away from her computer to write a thesis. Theses are held dear by Lutherans because of Martin Luther's *Ninety-Five*. Her thesis will explain to her father why she wants to leave Saint Olaf College and attend the University of Wisconsin at Milwaukee in the fall. She writes:

"Saint Olaf is an excellent college with a great faculty and students who are very polite to me. But unlike my years at Lakeville North High School I find that I have no close friends in Northfield. I think that it is fair for me to write this after four semesters there. I have given the school a good try, the old college try, so to speak. I know that it is I, and not the school that has the problem. I am a square peg trying to fit into a round hole and I am lonely, Dad, very lonely. When I took the Greyhound to visit the Mathematics Department of the University of Wisconsin at Milwaukee I felt at peace. I saw plenty of students who look like me all over the campus, groups of them. People said hello to me and gave me directions when I was looking for the math building."

Erma pauses because she is crying. She reaches for a Kleenex from the box on Dorothy's desk to wipe her eyes and blow her nose. Cameron walks out of his office, carrying a novel by Vince Flynn. Cameron loves Mitch Rapp, the main character in most of Flynn's novels.

"Erma, you're crying," Cameron says.

"I know Mr. Kills Pretty Enemy."

"Why are you crying?"

"Because …"

And then the telephone rings. Cameron raises his hand, stopping her explanation as the two of them listen to the three long rings that happen before the answering machine is activated. They stare at the phone. Erma reaches for the legal pad and a pen. A voice comes through the speaker.

"Good afternoon," a woman says. "I am leaving this message for Cameron Kills Pretty Enemy. Cameron, this is Iris Murphy."

Erma writes all of this down, ignoring Cameron.

The woman stops and makes the hiccupping sound that comes when a person is trying not to cry. Cameron puts down the Vince Flynn novel and sits in Dorothy's chair. He stares at the answering machine.

"The thing is Cameron I don't really care if your office manager hears this message so I will just say it. I am dying. The oncologist gives me two months. But our mutual friend, Paul, says that that is what all oncologists tell people in dire circumstances to motivate action. Needless to say it has motivated me. I want to ask you to continue to stay in contact with Miles and to call me at 402-341-2173. I want to say goodbye to you and I want to ask you 'Why?' Why do you refuse to communicate with me? That's what I have always wondered. Was it because I'm white? Was it my politics? Was it my religion? Did you love me at all? I love you. My dad said a person should end every conversation with love. I do …"

The answering machine stops every message at an ellipsis. Erma keeps transcribing. She finishes the transcription to the yellow pad from memory and then she begins to weep. Everyone, she thinks, works from the same broken heart. She looks up from the page. Cameron is crying. She pulls three Kleenexes from Dorothy's box and hands them to her cousin and then pulls three more for herself.

"Why don't you head home early, Erma," Cameron says, his red eyes looking away from her. "We'll still pay you for the last hour."

"You don't pay me, Mr. Kills Pretty Enemy."

"We don't?"

"No, I'm an unpaid intern."

"What about the other interns? The ones who carry my bags?"

"You don't pay them either."

"Oh."

"You need to call her," Erma tells him. "You need to do it right away. This is an emergency."

"Why were you crying, Erma?"

"Because I'm going to disappoint my dad. I'm going to move to Milwaukee to study at the University of Wisconsin because people look more like me there," Erma says this as she thinks "His name is Miles and his mother is dying" and she begins to cry again.

"Don't cry. Going to Milwaukee will be a good thing for you."

"But if a white man loved me and in loving him I became a better person I would marry him."

She blows her nose.

"It's never that simple."

Erma reaches for her backpack.

"Your dad loves you very much. He will always be proud of you."

"Do the right thing, Mr. Kills Pretty Enemy."

"I'll see you next week."

Erma nods her head.

"I'll pay you."

"You should pay all of your interns."

Cameron winces.

"Dorothy wouldn't approve of that."

On the drive back to Northfield, Erma replays the woman's message to Cameron over in her head and she wonders if Miles knows that his mother is dying and how Cameron came to know Iris Murphy and if he is still in love with her and why he won't speak to her. She recites the phone number aloud. Numbers are her true language. They soothe her busy mind and carry none of the burden of subjectivity. It is subjective to find herself sympathetic to Cameron's obvious grief and simultaneously angered by his refusal to comfort the sick.

When she reaches the Saint Olaf lot where is she permitted to park Erma pulls out her iPhone. She presses the ten digits into the keypad. Two seconds pass before she hears the phone ring.

"Hello," a woman's voice answers the phone after the second ring.

"Good afternoon, this is Erma Charging. I work as an intern in the law office of Cameron Kills Pretty Enemy and I am calling for Iris Murphy."

"This is Iris Murphy."

"Ms. Murphy, I think it is important for you to know that Mr. Kills Pretty Enemy never takes calls on Wednesday."

"Yes."

"But sometimes he listens to what comes over the answering machine."

"Yes."

"Mr. Kills Pretty Enemy listened to your message today."

"Will he be calling me?"

"Well, I cannot say for certain, but I think not ..."

Then Erma hears a stifled cry.

"However I would like to tell you that Mr. Kills Pretty Enemy did cry as he listened to your words and that he loves Miles very much. He keeps pictures of him in the office on Wednesdays."

"What did you say your name is?"

"My name is Erma Charging."

"Ms. Charging, you do know that you could lose your job for calling me?"

"Ms. Murphy, I'm an unpaid intern. I wouldn't be losing very much and none of the other interns are interested in working on Excel spreadsheets or updating the website. They all want to be attorneys."

"What do you want to be, Ms. Charging?"

No one ever asks Erma this question. As a pastor's child her family life has been focused on other people's needs. Someone always needs her father or needs something as basic as food or shelter. Erma realizes that she has grown up on the good side of greater than. There is an implied frivolousness to admitting that she has wants in a world where so many people live with far less than what they need. Christ did not die on a cross for humanity's wants.

"I want to go to the University of Wisconsin at Milwaukee to major in mathematics and then see what happens."

"You should do it."

"I will."

And Erma Charging knows now that she will.

"Thank you for calling me. I will tell no one about our conversation."

"You will be in my prayers, Ms. Murphy."

"And you in mine, Ms. Charging."

The conversation ends.

Erma begins to weep for this woman and her son, and for Milwaukee. Her tears fall in grief, joy, and relief. Her prayer is for grace for them all.

Students walk through the parking lot. Their eyes are on smart phones or behind sunglasses. Classes are over. Tomorrow is Reading Day. It is the season of beginnings. They are good children of kind people, but they do not see Erma Charging who is sobbing against her steering wheel. And they never will.

Ferragamo

It is still dark in Cincinnati as Dr. Ezra Holloway backs the Aerostar down the driveway. He waves to his wife who stands beneath the streetlight, holding the hand of their two and half-year-old son. Charlie is still in his sleepers and Anna in her bathrobe. Mother and child wave to the people and the dog inside the van.

Ezra can see his Maine coon cat, Horace Mann, peering down on their departure. A halo of artificial light outlines his beloved pet as the cat sits in the window of the front landing of their home. Erect in posture, with his marmalade-colored tail wrapped around his feet, Horace offers the public a dignified image, but Ezra knows that the cat is not happy. He can feel the scowl emanating from within the deep recesses of the feline's heart.

At first, Horace hated Boots. He hissed at the dog in a puffed up fashion whenever they came into contact with one another. Then Horace chose to ignore him walking out of a space each time the canine entered it. When a month had passed, and Boots was still living with the family, Horace took on a look of studied indifference to him so long as Boots never sat at Ezra's feet. Boots learned quickly to sit a respectful distance from the cat and the man when all were in the same room together. The dog never quarreled with the fact that Dr. Ezra Holloway belonged to the big, orange feline. He acknowledged the reality that Horace owned Ezra.

After more than a year in the company of Boots, it became apparent to all that the older cat's grudging tolerance for the younger dog had grown into a reluctant affection. Maine coon cats, in general, are very tolerant creatures, even of dogs. Though Horace Mann is, by personality, the least tolerant of his breed, given time, he will tip toward a form of peaceful co-existence. Over the years, Horace has learned to accept Anna and to endure the now fast-moving toddler, Charlie, though he will never understand why Ezra brought them into the household in the first place. The cat considers Ezra his chosen human. All others are secondary, sometimes even tertiary, in his affections.

As a veterinarian Ezra knows that Boots is a survivor. The dog's ability to adapt, which is probably related to his mixed breed heritage, has given him the acumen to size up a situation. Boots acquiesced to the cat's dominant nature. Horace Mann likes to be the boss, even if only in appearance. The blessing for the household is that the dog loves to labor. Whether it is on the long runs he takes with Ezra down Erie Avenue, or his watchful presence when he walks with Anna and Charlie through Hyde Park Square, Boots has been there to serve and protect. At night, he sleeps in his dog bed at the foot of the stairs across from the front door. His ear is cocked for the wrong night sounds — a human footstep, a city rat, or a meandering raccoon. The low growl that resounds from his broad chest signifies to prospective trespassers a bite that is far worse than his bark.

In four days everything has changed for the Holloway family on Saint Charles Place. A glance at a text upended things as Ezra presumed they were going to be in his household, at least regarding their pets. The message on his smart phone did more than startle him it frightened him.

"Aunt Iris has been threatened by a very bad man," Bridget Murphy-Holloway wrote to her son. "SHE NEEDS A DOG NOW!!!"

Of course what his mom wanted to type was "SHE NEEDS BOOTS," but she knew that her son and daughter-in-law had grown to love the animal that had appeared one day in their front yard. What his mom didn't know is that her son would never make the dog move to Omaha. It was up to Boots to decide.

Before talking to Boots, Ezra spoke with Horace Mann. Horace was looking out the landing's window at the soft greens of late April and at the redbud tree in bloom across the cul-de-sac. Sitting next to the cat on the window seat, Ezra described the situation.

"Aunt Iris lives alone in a very large house, Horace, and someone has threatened to harm her."

Horace moved his shoulders as if he were shrugging, as if he were saying to Ezra, "So what?" The cat seemed entirely unenthusiastic to the plight of Iris Murphy.

In his mind's eye, Ezra could see a collage of black and white images of the dog and cat together when the Holloway humans were away from the house.

Then Horace made a plaintive chirrup that sounded like the words, "My dog."

"My aunt is ill," Ezra added. "She has cancer. Aunt Iris needs Boots."

Horace turned his head away from the scene beyond the windowpanes to give Ezra a look of resignation and a chirp that sounded to Ezra like defeat.

Later that day at the end of a long run Ezra told Boots about his mother's request for a dog for her sister.

"I would have to take you to Omaha, Boots, and it is faraway from Cincinnati. You wouldn't be living with us anymore."

Speaking these words left Ezra bereft. Tears spilled down his face, merging into the rivulets of runner's sweat on his T-shirt. Ezra hugged the dog, knowing that he would never force Boots to go to Omaha, if he did not want to go.

Boots, however, was reflective. Images of Horace Mann flooded into Ezra's thoughts, leading him to say,

"Horace Mann won't be going to Omaha, Boots, only you would go. You would be living with Aunt Iris, just the two of you. My cousin, Miles, will visit, but he doesn't live in Omaha anymore."

The dog's jaw dropped into a canine expression of a smile. Ezra understood, then, that Boots wanted a home of his own, free from Horace's tyranny. He did not tell the old cat that Boots was going to Omaha because the dog wanted to go. He let Horace think that the dog was going because Ezra needed him to protect his aunt. Boots did nothing to dissuade Horace from this point-of-view. Neither Ezra nor the dog wanted the cat's feelings hurt.

The trip was organized quickly. Ezra's mother requested family leave from Saint Rita School for the Deaf and his father re-scheduled several piano tunings. Colleagues are covering for Ezra at the clinic as well. While both of his parents look pensive behind their seatbelts, Boots looks, if a dog can look this way, thrilled. Companion animals long for their singular person and Horace Mann has Ezra. Boots now knows that he is getting his in Iris Murphy.

Ezra tunes the radio to WGUC as he turns the van onto Erie Avenue. The "Nimrod" portion of Edward Elgar's *Enigma Variations* plays as they drive into the pale beginnings of morning. He glances into the rearview mirror. His dad's eyes are closed as he listens to the music. Boots, who is strapped into the seat next to Walter Holloway, looks out the window at the neighborhood that he is now leaving. Ezra's mother, who is in the passenger seat next to him, touches the dashboard to feel the music's vibrations. Bridget Murphy-Holloway smiles and signs to her son,

"Your dad loves classical music."

Ezra nods his head.

The three humans and the dog make their way from Interstate 71 north to the Norwood Lateral west to Interstate 75 south until they merge onto Interstate 74 west going towards Indiana. It is a trip they know well. A portion of every summer of his boyhood, Ezra spent in Omaha with his aunt Iris, his grandparents, and his cousin Miles. His mom and dad would drive him there, and two weeks later they would return to bring him home. Ezra loves Omaha.

Children can only know what they experience and what Ezra learned growing up was that his parents, Walter and Bridget, adored each other and him. He was in fourth grade before he gave much thought to the fact of his father's skin color or his mother's deafness. It was the year that his elementary school covered slavery, the Civil War and Helen Keller. They called the course history. Even then Ezra thought of history like spaghetti, looping itself endlessly around into the present. He felt that way when his cousin Miles told him,

"My dad is a full-blooded Lakota Indian."

"Like with the cowboys?"

"Yeah."

"Does he have a horse?"

"I don't know."

It is the reality of only and cosseted children to be frank in their thoughts. Neither he nor Miles were trained to be afraid of the world. However, the boys' constant observation of adults made them more cautious than daring, at least until their teenage years. Their adored grandfather, Jack Murphy, was probably a perfect specimen of Attention Deficit Hyperactivity Disorder as a young man. Thirty years of fighting Omaha's fires drained him of his lack of focus. He learned to pay attention. And, of course, there were Jack Murphy's beautiful daughters, one of whom was deaf. Grandpa Jack adored his daughters and he revered his wife, but he worried about those girls. It could be said that the Murphy girls gave their father a run for his money.

"Be sure of this, boys, God has a sense of humor," Grandpa Jack once told Ezra and Miles when reflecting on being the father of females.

Ezra presumes that Grandpa Jack never expected to have two such dark-skinned grandchildren, but his grandfather never spoke to those kinds of issues. He was far more interested in showing his grandsons how to use power tools, or taking them to see the giraffes at the Henry Doorly Zoo, than discussing politics, race relations, or God forbid, sex. Grandpa Jack gave Ezra his first dog, but never a sip of beer or a cigarette.

His grandfather's diagnosis of lung cancer while Ezra was at veterinary school should not have stunned him, but it did. From his hospital bed Jack Murphy said to him,

"Thank God for the cancer, Ezra, because I hate this emphysema."

He died quickly of a firefighter's diseases. Soon afterwards Ezra's grandmother Honora died of congestive heart failure. There were many that said the cause was heartbreak. Jack and Honora liked to be together. This could not be denied.

"What did your mom say about the cancer?" his cousin Miles asked him by Skype two days before the departure to Omaha.

"Mom says that the oncologist in Omaha wants Aunt Iris to get a second opinion and that she's going to Minnesota for it."

Miles grimaced and then said,

"Mom likes to shop in the Twin Cities. There is no tax on clothing there. Hopefully, she'll make it to her doctor's appointment. What do you think, Ezra?"

"I don't know, Miles. There's so much that they can do these days. Oncology is a specialty even in veterinary science."

"Mom says that the doctors want to do this de-bulking surgery after they shrink the tumors with the oral oncology. What's there to de-bulk on my mother? She's so little already."

From his apartment in Nairobi, Miles looked shaken. Ezra wanted to tell him that it would all be okay and that his mom would get better. Instead he hedged his bets by telling him the truth.

"When we get to Omaha I'll talk to her. But I really don't know much about her diagnosis at this point. We learned about the threats and the cancer at the same time and I guess I've been focusing on getting Boots to Omaha."

"Thank you for the dog."

"Boots will protect her, Miles. No one will get near her when he's around."

"I don't want my mom to die."

Then his big cousin covered his face and began to cry. Ezra watched him through the computer screen feeling helpless. Though Aunt Iris is small she has always felt larger than life to Ezra. Small dogs generally outlive big dogs and Aunt Iris has the fierce spirit of a Yorkshire terrier. She is a giant slayer.

When Ezra was twelve and Miles ten their grandparents took the boys to court to watch Aunt Iris defend a man who was charged with possession of cocaine with intent to distribute. The man's name was Jesus. The Omaha police had stopped him on a traffic violation late one winter evening. They searched the car and found the cocaine in the seat cushions. Later the police questioned Jesus, reading him his Miranda rights in English, a language that Jesus did not speak well. They charged him and put him in the Douglas County jail. There he sat for three weeks because he could not make bail or hire an attorney.

The Douglas County Public Defender's Office assigned Iris Murphy to his case. Through a translator Aunt Iris learned that the car did not belong to Jesus. His cousin had loaned it to him for the night. The translator told Aunt Iris that Jesus had no idea that there was cocaine sewn into the back seat cushions of the car. The Douglas County attorney's office offered a Jesus a deal involving jail time, but Aunt Iris advised her client that they should go to court. If Jesus accepted the prosecutor's offer he would lose his green card after serving his sentence and be forced to leave the United States when released from prison. All of this Nana Honora explained to Ezra as they drove to the courthouse.

Ezra had heard his aunt practicing her defense in the laundry room the night before the trial.

"Iris always practices," his grandmother told Ezra when he asked her about what she was doing.

 Ezra remembers watching as Iris Murphy took apart the evidence offered by the prosecutor. She did it, point-by-point, respectfully and neatly. She put Jesus on the stand and through a translator he told his story. His cousin, he explained, was taking care of the car for a man who had moved out of town. Jesus had borrowed the Ford Escort from his cousin because his car had broken down the night before.

"Where were you going in the car?"

Through a translator Jesus said,

"I was going to work at Bergen Mercy Hospital. I work in the kitchen washing dishes."

Then Aunt Iris entered into evidence that Jesus had been employed as a dishwasher in the kitchen of Bergen Mercy Hospital. He was scheduled to work that night. The police officer had stopped him on Mercy Road not far from the hospital's entrance.

When Aunt Iris questioned the arresting police officer she asked him why he had pulled over the car.

"His tail light on the passenger side was out. It was after dark."

Aunt Iris then showed the court that the Ford Escort was titled to another man. She also entered into evidence that this man had convictions for possession of marijuana. When Jesus was stopped he had given the officer a valid Nebraska driver's license and the green card that allowed him to work. (There was no registration in the car or valid stickers on the license plates, a point made earlier by the prosecutor.)

The trial was over before lunch. When the foreman read aloud the words "Not guilty," and then the words were translated into Spanish Jesus sobbed. The members of the jury looked relieved, as did the judge.

Aunt Iris and her client were the first to walk out of the courtroom.

Ezra watched the police officer give his aunt the stink-eye, but she did not seem to care. Looking pissed the prosecutor avoided the eyes of the cop as he followed the translator out the door.

Ezra, Miles, and his grandparents exited the small courtroom before the next trial was called to order. They watched as his aunt spoke to Jesus through the translator. When Jesus left surrounded by his family the prosecutor called out,

"Iris," in an irritated voice.

"Yes, Mr. Manning."

"You should work on our side."

"Good day, Mr. Manning."

"I mean it."

"I know."

That night Ezra's grandparents celebrated his aunt's victory by getting carryout at the Popeye's Fried Chicken on Dodge Street. They ate their dinner on the picnic table in the backyard. Grandpa Jack and Nana Honora each drank a bottle of Budweiser and smoked two Camel cigarettes apiece. The family did not discuss the trial.

In the middle of the night Ezra awoke to hear someone vomiting in the bathroom down the hall. Miles was also awake.

"Who's that?" he asked his cousin.

"It's Mom."

"Do you think it was the Popeye's?"

"No, Mom always gets sick after trials," Miles said from his place on the bottom bunk. "She's frightened that she'll lose. If she loses then her client will get a much worse sentence then if she had accepted the plea deal offered by the prosecutor. Most of her work is deals."

"The guy was innocent," Ezra remembers saying to Miles then. "You'd have to be a moron not to know that from the evidence she presented."

"The guy was Mexican and you never know how it's going to go. It all depends on the makeup of the jury and what's in their hearts. That's what Mom says. A cop would have stopped a white guy with a tail light out, but there's no way he would have searched the car that way, poking at the seat cushions."

Miles said this in a very matter-of-fact voice. He sounded like an experienced trial watcher rather than a ten-year-old. Ezra was startled by the injustice of it all. Even now his pulse begins to race when he thinks of his aunt in the courtroom that day with so much depending on her.

Ezra's aunt leaves nothing to chance. She dresses carefully, beautifully. Before she speaks she thinks. Aunt Iris never rushes into her words. People hang in her pauses, waiting for what she is going to say.

Only in adulthood has Ezra begun to wonder about the physical cost of such a calm demeanor and how it can deplete energy, increasing stress. This he learned from caring for cats. Felines will feign health, until they are near death, rather than let the harsh world know of their weakened state. Predators make short work of an ill cat.

In and around the courthouse it would seem that his aunt did not care what others thought of her, but, of course, Ezra thinks, she did. Ezra has not forgotten that night of her retching and how pale she looked the next morning. She left for Mass as everyone else was eating breakfast.

Aunt Iris is a daily communicant, leaving home early so that she can attend Mass at the Church of Saint Mary Magdalene before work.

Ezra remembers how she would pray in church on Sundays. She knelt in the pew with her eyes shut and her forehead against her clasped hands. Ezra could see her lips moving silently. Aunt Iris prayed far longer than any other adult in the family. One time as they walked out of Saint Margaret Mary Church, Ezra asked his grandmother,

"Why does she pray like that, Nana?"

"Our Iris has prayed like that since she was a little girl. She prays for you and Miles and your mother and your father and she prays for

Jack and me. She prays for the world and peace and for the people who walk into her office wanting help. Her clients are always somewhat guilty, I suppose, but aren't we all? The squeaky wheels get God's grease, or at least that's what I hope."

Ezra wonders what his aunt prays for now as he sees the sign for Champaign, Illinois. His mother, whose hands speak, almost constantly, has had little to say on this road trip.

"Look, I'll Skype with you as soon as I get the lay of the land in Omaha," he told Miles as their conversation drew to a close.

Miles nodded and then said,

"I was planning to tell you next month when I'm back the States, but I will now. I'm getting married. Margaret said 'Yes.' I want you to be my best man."

"That's great news! Congratulations! I'm honored."

Miles grinned.

"Thanks," Miles said, and then paused.

Ezra waited.

"I need to ask a favor of you. Mom should sell the house. Can you bring that up, Ezra? The whole world knows where she lives because of the political signs she puts up there. She'll have a sign as big as a barn for Obama in the front yard, you can bet on that. Of course, crazies are going to threaten her. How can she take care of that big house and her health?"

"I'll try, but you know how the Murphy girls feel about that house."

Miles sighed.

"I promise I'll try," he said again.

"Thank you."

The trip is uneventful. They park at rest stops for Boots and his mother to the use the facilities in Indiana and Illinois. They eat lunch on a plaza outside of a McDonald's in Davenport, Iowa so the dog can be with them. Ezra can smell the soil and its scent of growing things. They cross the Missouri River, driving into Omaha at a little past five o'clock Central Standard Time. His mom texts Aunt Iris, letting her know that they soon will be there.

When they turn the corner onto Cass Street the van drives under an arc of old trees leafed out in gradations of green. Bridal wreath and lilacs in full bloom surround the houses. Walter Holloway begins to laugh and Bridget to smile. Then Ezra sees the "Obama Biden 2012" sign in his aunt's yard. The sign is not the size of a barn, but it looks as large as a refrigerator turned on its side.

"Iris, Iris," his dad says aloud.

"It's so good to be home," his mom signs to him with a sigh.

After nearly forty years in Cincinnati, Bridget Murphy-Holloway still longs for Omaha.

As Ezra pulls up on the driveway Aunt Iris, her friend Martha, and the man Ezra knows as "Uncle Paul" all walk out of the back door. A white-haired man, Ezra does not know, follows Paul. Walter slides back the van door, leaving Boots belted in place and then he opens the door for his wife. Together they go to meet the welcoming committee. Ezra's mom hugs her sister and then Martha while his dad shakes the hands of the two men. Hands fly and the chatter begins.

"This is your new home, Boots," Ezra tells the dog from behind the steering wheel before getting out of the van.

Ezra goes around the vehicle to slide back the passenger door. Getting inside he sits next to Boots and attaches a sturdy leash to the dog's thick leather collar. Then he puts a Gentle Leader around Boots' muzzle before releasing the seatbelt. They get out together. He walks the dog into the front yard and under the walnut tree. Boots lifts his leg and takes a good long leak.

"Good dog, Boots," Ezra tells him.

Then Aunt Iris walks up to Ezra and Boots with a water dish that she puts at the dog's feet. As the dog drinks, Ezra wraps his free arm around her well-dressed frame. The day is in the high seventies and the sun will be with them until well past seven o'clock. Aunt Iris is dressed in layers of silver and gray — a cotton shirt, linen pants, a linen jacket, and a fuchsia-colored scarf knotted at her throat. The loveliness of her clothing distracts the viewer from noticing her size. Always a small woman she is now even smaller. Ezra's big left arm holds her to him. He can hear her swift beating heart. She feels like a captured bird, something that could be broken, with little or no pressure. There is nothing to her.

"Hello, my favorite nephew."

"I'm your only nephew."

"Yet and still you are greatest nephew in the world."

"You are the finest aunt in the universe and all universes beyond this one."

She smiles.

Ezra kisses the silver crown of her head. She touches his cheek. They stand with their arms around one another watching the dog without words. Black and white images flow from Boots to Ezra — the woman, the house, the people standing on the driveway, his food dish, even a smudged vision of Horace Mann. Ezra and his aunt wait as the dog sizes up his situation. Iris Murphy does not bend down to Boots. She waits for him to come to her. The animal must understand who is boss. Everyone in the yard grows silent, watching the introductions.

Minutes pass before Boots leaves the water dish to sit in front of Iris Murphy. Ezra hands her the leash. Aunt Iris offers the dog her right fist. He sniffs it. The hand opens. Boots eats the kibble from her palm.

"Good dog," she says. "I will call you Ferragamo, Boots. It's a name of beauty for you my handsome dog."

Ezra can feel the dog falling in love with the woman who has given him the dignity of a great name. The dog understands only what he can perceive — the yard, the kibble, the water bowl, a house — all of this will be his. In an instant the veterinarian knows that the woman next to him is dying. It is the science of his training. He feels this realization like a stab in his gut as his aunt pets the dog's head, cooing the words, "Ferragamo, Ferragamo."

"Aunt Iris."

"Ezra."

"You're …"

She raises her open palm to him, stopping him, punctuating it with a lift of her eyebrow.

"You must know that I'm throwing every Hail Mary pass that I can, Ezra."

"But …"

She shakes her head and then whispers,

"I'm trying my best to get well, but chemotherapy doesn't seem to agree with me. Do you understand?"

Ezra nods his head, wanting to say that chemotherapy rarely agrees with anyone, as far as he knows, but he does not.

"I don't think I'll be up to the de-bulking surgery. But this, of course, is between you and me."

"And the dog," Ezra says, but he is thinking about Miles, and what he has promised him.

Aunt Iris nods her head and then hugs Boots now Ferragamo.

"You, of course, won't say anything to Miles."

Ezra does not respond, because he has always told Miles everything and his allegiance is to his cousin more so than to his aunt.

"Ezra, this is my story, not yours."

She says this to him as though he has violated a HIPAA privacy document. She says it like an attorney. This, he knows, he will hold against her and even as he thinks it he feels guilty. She is a dying woman. She has rights.

"Aunt Iris …"

"No, I mean it. This is my life and you cannot tell this to Miles before I'm ready to deal with it."

Her eyes are snapping with the power of the Vikings who raped and plundered Ireland, leaving the island with the fierce blue-gray irises that she has turned on him. For a moment Ezra empathizes with all the prosecutors who have lost to Iris Murphy and the men whose hearts she has broken, or so his mother has told him.

"But ..."

"I will tell him soon enough."

Ezra wants to say, "This is not just your story," but he can't. He won't, because he has no idea what dying feels like. And he loves her. She has never asked anything of him except for this, and his dog.

"Ferragamo," she says to the dog. "You need to meet my friends and claim your new home."

His aunt leads the dog away from him. Ezra stands staring at the Obama-Biden sign, composing himself as he always does when he has bad news to give to the families of the animals he cares for.

"Your composure will offer them hope," his professors claimed.

Later, he will cry in the shower for the loss of his dog, and for his aunt. The mysterious Iris Murphy.

The Awkward Made Beautiful

Sᴇʀɢᴇᴀɴᴛ Cʟᴀʏᴛᴏɴ Sᴀɴᴛᴏs-Aɴᴅᴇʀsᴏɴ sɪᴛs ᴀᴄʀᴏss a small table from Iris Murphy at a bistro called Mark's a few blocks from Ms. Murphy's house in the Dundee neighborhood of Omaha. They are seated beside a window. It is late in July of 2012. The dog days have not yet begun, but the weather is quite warm and the dew point high. Everyone in Omaha seems to be out-of-town. They have traveled to cool places with deep lakes or high mountains. Clayton feels like he owns the city on weekends like this.

"Sergeant Santos-Anderson," Ms. Murphy says, leaning in to show him something on the menu. "I think you might like this."

"I'll have that," Clayton responds, looking up to the server, and then he realizes that he has no idea what he will be eating, because he had only glanced at the words on the page so that they could be finished with the ritual of ordering. What he saw, actually, was Ms. Murphy's delicate index finger below some fuzzy print. His reading glasses are in his shirt pocket.

For Clayton the pleasure of the meal is being with Ms. Murphy again. The food, he knows, will be fine. He is not picky, but she seems to be. Underneath the table, he can feel her small kneecap occasionally leaning into his leg and then retreating.

Clayton has spent the morning driving around Fair Acres. In April, there were reports of a well-dressed older woman visiting open houses in this upscale neighborhood of the city. After the woman's visits small and expensive objects were reported missing by the homeowners to their realtors.

"She has an eye for things of value that most people know nothing about," a seller told Clayton. "Most people think my stuff is clutter. Well, at least, my kids do. I didn't think to worry. Who in Omaha would know?"

What the realtors remembered about the perpetrator was that she drove a vintage Mercedes Benz that was yellow, or possibly green, and that her well-mannered grandsons were with her. These realtors were not clear about the number of children. One says that there were three kids and another says there was only one. They did agree on the fact that the children were boys and that they were wearing khakis. The lone boy was said to be wearing a Madras shirt, but the three boys were all wearing blue blazers with their chinos. No one could remember any names being shared.

By May 1, the reports stopped. The Mercedes was not to be seen on Omaha's streets. But in the past week, two realtors have left voicemail messages for Clayton with sightings of the vintage vehicle. He is back in the hunt.

Fair Acres adjoins Dundee, so when Clayton realized that he would not be far from Ms. Murphy's house he called her. Ostensibly the call was professional in nature, even though he would be meeting with Ms. Murphy on his day off. After lunch his plan is to look around the grounds of her house to check for signs of forced entry, or places that could be opened easily. Many locks are poorly designed and criminals know them all. They also know that distracted homeowners often forget to lock their doors. Some burglars only enter unlocked homes. They never waste their time on fiddling with locks, breaking glass, or cutting screens. Clayton wants to remind Ms. Murphy about these realities, but mostly he wants to see her. She is often in his thoughts, and when he remembers to pray, his prayers.

"Sergeant Santos-Anderson, I'm so glad to hear your voice," she said to him.

"And, I, yours."

After he explained his reason for calling, she asked him,

"Have you ever been to Mark's Bistro?"

"No, Ms. Murphy."

"I will take you there. I think you will love it."

And here they are.

As Iris Murphy looks out the window Clayton studies her profile. Her blue eyes are bright, above more pronounced cheekbones. She has lost weight. Her silver hair is pushed behind her ears and a strand of blush-colored pearls dip in and out of the crevice created by the two buttons opened at the top of her black cotton cardigan.

"The air conditioning is so cold," she says with a slight quaver in her voice. Then she pulls a red scarf from her handbag and loops it around her neck.

To everyone in the restaurant she is a lovely woman of an indeterminate age — above fifty — but where above fifty? More importantly she does not look like she is dying. This is important to Clayton. He is ashamed at his discomfort with death, but nonetheless the subject disturbs him. When he thinks about Ms. Murphy he focuses on her getting well. She is deserving of a medical miracle and supposedly they happen every day. He blinks back the sensation of tears and turns his gaze away from her to the treetops in the distance. Hope for Clayton is green.

After Ms. Murphy left the Omaha Police Department that day in April Clayton filed his report and called the penitentiary in Lincoln with Leonard Howard's accusations regarding Angelo Bartlett. It turned out that Bartlett was no longer in the care of the State of Nebraska's correctional system. He had been paroled two weeks earlier to a halfway house in Omaha. After a series of phone calls and emails the investigation began. First, it moved slowly and then quickly. It seemed that no one could quite believe that Angelo Bartlett would have held any grudge against Iris Murphy. It made no sense to them because Iris had never represented Angelo Bartlett, nor had she ever declined to defend him. But reason, they all agreed among themselves, has little to do with the motivation of most criminals, certainly not someone like Angelo Bartlett.

Eventually the prison investigator learned that what the deaf-mute Leonard Howard had confided in Ms. Murphy about the sign language among prisoners was true. Anonymous sources reported that Angelo hated how Ms. Murphy reached out to teenage prostitutes, helping them find shelter, employment, and counseling.

"Once she helped get one of his girls off the streets," a prisoner reported.

"Bartlett hates the way Iris Murphy puts pamphlets in the public defender's office. It gives the girls ideas," someone anonymously scrawled across a sheet of paper left on a table in the prison library.

Two men indicated that there was a plan to damage her house and possibly to leave threatening notes.

"Because it will scare her," one said.

"He'll get kids to do it. They'll do anything for a little cash or drugs."

With this information the Omaha Police Department obtained a warrant on the first Wednesday in May and sent a cruiser to Mr. Bartlett's residence on a short block cut into the side of a hill in South Omaha, but he had already left for work. When they arrived at the warehouse where Angelo worked disassembling desktop and laptop computers for an electronics recycling company they were directed to the employee lunchroom where Angelo was supposed to be taking his break. He was not there. His broken ankle monitor was later found in the staff microwave.

If life were a suspense novel then Angelo Bartlett would have been in the process of making his way to Iris Murphy's home at the same time as the police discovered that he had bolted. Reaching her house, he would have jimmied a lock and silently entered the building where he would have waited to attack Ms. Murphy while she was doing something domestic, private, and ordinary. The novelist's descriptions of the heinous and brutal things carried out by Angelo would bring about a peculiar thrill in a certain kind of reader, and possibly in the author as well. Or another plot summary would have the police showing up, just in time, to rescue her. Ms. Murphy would have been terrorized, possibly assaulted, but saved. Life, however, is rarely a work of psychological suspense, or experienced along the lines of a police procedural. And thank goodness for that, Clayton thinks, as he looks across the bistro. He does not read books with the arc of fear and violence built into them. The resolutions never feel resolved to him. There is always a hot mess of problems after a serious crime that can echo down a family for decades. He has no idea why people like these kinds of books. Many police officers do enjoy them and this puts Clayton in the minority. However he is not uncomfortable being different and he knows this to be one of his strengths. It is why he has made his career in Property Crime.

Instead of searching for Iris Murphy, Angelo Bartlett walked to downtown Omaha and then across the Missouri River via the Bob Kerrey Pedestrian Bridge to arrive in Council Bluffs, Iowa. With thirty dollars in his pocket he went looking for a gambling establishment and found one quickly on a riverboat. A woman sitting next to Angelo at the slot machines took a shine to him. She bought him a meal at the buffet and a considerable amount of alcohol before they left the casino together. They proceeded to further enjoy one another's company in the backseat of her 2003 Cadillac Seville where they fell asleep. When the woman awoke to see Mr. Bartlett rifling through her fake Prada handbag she reached into one of the hidden compartments that General

Motors has so kindly put into this luxury vehicle to pull out a small, but well-maintained pearl handled revolver.

"He didn't even notice I was awake," she told a Council Bluffs police officer. "I shot the bastard in his ass. And once in the leg, so he couldn't walk away, at least not comfortably. Then I pulled out my cell phone and called 911, as he hightailed it out of the car."

Angelo Bartlett held onto the purse. He did not toss it as he limped through the parking lot. The arresting officers found it in his hands when they apprehended him five blocks from the scene of the crime. The woman may not have been lucky in love that night, but she made up for that by having the sense to hold onto her rather sizable winnings from the blackjack tables. Mr. Bartlett's current injuries and crimes are now in the hands of Iowa's authorities. The residents of Pottawattamie County will be footing his bill for longer than they will want. Eventually they will get him off of their books and back to Lincoln, Nebraska for parole and other violations.

When members of the Omaha Police Department learned of Leonard Howard's connection to the apprehension of Angelo Bartlett there was a sense that possibly, just possibly, Leonard Howard was capable of doing a good deed. The police, locally, and nationally, are relentlessly unforgiving of harm done to police officers or their families. Leonard's reputation as an unrepentant drunk who backed into a cop with his car will never be forgiven, but because he tried to help Iris Murphy, for no reason other than to help her, gave the cops something to ponder. Two weeks later Leonard keeled over in the prison library. A man, who most of the force believe should not be in prison at all, Kenneth Yellow Dog, helped the librarian give Leonard CPR, as the deaf man was dying.

The cops like the zoo. They also like to eat beef and think highly of the Cattlemen's Association, the group that wanted Yellow Dog prosecuted, but they thought it was a damn shame that Yellow Dog was sent to Lincoln. Most of the Omaha Police Department, including Clayton, thinks that Kenneth Yellow Dog should be released immediately. The only thing he ever did was to sleep with the giraffes at the zoo and even the cops didn't think that that was such a big deal. Yellow Dog did not steal the little donkey or the miniature horses, his parents did. It didn't take a genius to figure that out. But his parents are old and his father is not well. He went to jail so his parents wouldn't. That will forever be the story behind Kenneth Yellow Dog's imprisonment. He didn't trust the prosecutors to give his folks a fair deal. And really, why would any Native American trust a prosecutor? Clayton has thought this thought on more than one occasion. These kinds of thoughts are another reason why he is still in Property Crime.

Clayton's contact at the prison called him the day that Leonard Howard passed away to ask him if he would mind telling Iris Murphy about her friend's death.

"I don't want Ms. Murphy to read about it in the obituaries," she told Clayton. "Iris Murphy was the only person who ever visited Leonard Howard, besides his attorney. And Howard did her a good turn."

Clayton agreed to do this. He immediately called Ms. Murphy at the Douglas County Public Defender's Office and asked if he could stop by and see her. Within forty minutes he was sitting across the desk from Iris.

When he was a young police officer, Clayton had gone on three different calls to tell mothers that their sons had passed away. Two were teenage boys killed in car accidents. The other was a second grade child who was shot by his cousin when the two boys found a pistol in a bedside drawer. They were all preventable deaths. Things like using seatbelts or locking guns away, or hiring responsible babysitters were, of course, thoughts that ran through his mind as he and his partner approached the homes and work places of these women, but they were left unsaid. Accidents do happen, everyday. The grief that they met after delivering the facts of these situations was epoch, mournful, and loud.

Clayton felt helpless and hapless in the face of it.

"How do you feel?" his then wife, Darla, asked him after one of these calls.

"Terrible," was all he could think to say to her, as he opened a bottle of Pabst Blue Ribbon in the small kitchen of their apartment. Then he took his beer into the bathroom. After locking the door, he turned on the shower, drank his PBR, and bawled like a baby.

Clayton remembered these moments as he looked at Ms. Murphy who was finishing something on her laptop computer and he felt bereft. His heart had never hardened. Then he looked at the picture books on a small bookcase and at a wicker basket of plastic toys in primary colors. Around the room were photographs of Ms. Murphy and a boy from his babyhood to college graduation. The boy looked like he could be Mexican, or from one of the reservations. Maybe she had adopted him, Clayton thought, absorbed in the relative quiet of the space and the clicking of computer keys. Then he heard a small cough and he turned back to Ms. Murphy. She was wearing reading glasses. They rested on the bridge of her nose.

"What did you want to see me about, Sergeant Santos-Anderson?"

"My contact in Lincoln called me today, Ms. Murphy, with some sad news," he told her. "Your friend, Leonard Howard, passed away in the prison library. It would appear that he had suffered some kind of coronary episode. I'm very sorry."

Iris Murphy's hands began to move back and forth in the space between them. The signs her hands formed felt huge to Clayton and full of pain. Ms. Murphy looked away from him as tears began to roll down her face. Clayton handed her his ironed and clean handkerchief.

"A gentleman always offers his handkerchief to a lady," Yolanda Santos-Anderson told her son when he was growing up. "And it's always a clean handkerchief."

"But what if I need to blow my nose?"

"Carry Kleenex."

"Sergeant Santos-Anderson, can you take some vacation time?" Ms. Murphy asked him, when her hands finally came to a hard stop. "Or do you need to return to work?"

"I could," he said. "I mean I can. No, I mean I will. I'll call the department and let them know."

"Would you escort me to La Buvette?"

"Of course," he said, standing up and pulling out his BlackBerry. "I'll take this outside."

Clayton's supervisor approved his request to use the vacation time, but he laughed when he heard why Clayton would not be back in the department that day.

"You'll be drinking with the better half, Sergeant Santos-Anderson. Will you still want to be a cop tomorrow?"

These kinds of responses are the pain of telling the truth and Clayton knows this and again he answered honestly, "I would think so, Eddie."

Attorneys, professors from Omaha's universities, the creative types of the Old Market, and liberals with money drink at La Buvette, a wine bar and grocery store. Clayton had never darkened its doorway. He drove Ms. Murphy there in his F150. She ordered a bottle of French red wine and he requested a Stella Artois that he can't remember finishing. As she sipped her first glass of wine he changed from his uniform to jeans and a golf shirt in La Buvette's unpretentious men's room. (Cops always keep an extra set of street clothes in their trucks. This is another practical reality of being a police officer that few people know.)

Up some stairs and in the corner of the building, away from the door, Ms. Murphy told him how she came to love and be rejected by Leonard Howard and more than a decade later to have a child with a man who would never really speak to her again. Clayton realized that no one at the prison knew this back-story, nor did anyone at the public defender's office. He felt honored by her trust in him and he began to relax in their intimate corner next to boxes of pasta and bottles of cornichons.

"The Murphys tend to go against the grain," Ms. Murphy said on her third glass of wine.

They ordered something to eat.

Ms. Murphy asked him, "Are you from Omaha?"

"No," he said. "I'm from Saint Paul."

Ms. Murphy continued to ask him questions, like the attorney she is. It felt to Clayton that she truly wanted to know about him and his family, the pain of his divorce, how much he still misses his mother who now lives in Prior Lake near his brother the Lutheran minister, and how he adores his daughter, Maria. Again, Clayton noticed how beautifully dressed Ms. Murphy was. The pressed white blouse was fitted on a diagonal and her blue pencil skirt was businesslike, feminine, and almost provocative.

As they walked out of La Buvette and onto the cobblestones of the Old Market it was still daylight and Clayton remembers blinking. Ms. Murphy put her hand on his arm and then asked him,

"Could you give me a ride home, Sergeant Santos-Anderson? I'm not quite sober enough to drive. I can take the bus to work tomorrow. The guys at the parking lot know my car."

"Of course."

It was a short ride to her house. Silence filled the cab of the truck. All Clayton could think about was the stiffening between his legs. When he pulled up on the driveway he put the truck in park and turned off the engine. It was dusk and the cab of the truck was protected from a street view by an old walnut tree. They were hidden. Clayton thought about all this before kissing Iris Murphy. Her mouth opened and his tongue found hers. She tasted like red wine and flourless chocolate torte. They necked like teenagers. In the darkness her hand slipped in his pants and his hands into her push up bra and then the dog started barking.

"Oh, Ferragamo," she moaned.

"Ferragamo?" Clayton remembers sitting up, his stiffness receding.

"My dog. Ferragamo is worried about the truck and I need to let him out," she said, buttoning her blouse.

"Thank you, Sergeant Santos-Anderson, for everything. You're a lovely man."

"When can I see you again?"

"Darling," she sighed.

"What?"

"I have begun oncology. I shouldn't have had all that wine. I will pay for it tomorrow."

"I love you, Ms. Murphy."

"Oh, sweet man, you love me in the forgiving light of La Buvette. You're young and I'm not. There will be others in your future. Trust me."

"You're beautiful."

"You're kind," she whispered into his ear.

"I mean it."

"I'm dying."

"No."

"Yes, I think so," she said, opening the truck's door and giving him a small wave. "Please don't get out of the truck. It will upset Ferragamo."

Clayton began to cry as he put the truck in reverse.

The next morning he called Janousek Florist and ordered a dozen red roses for her. "Thank you, Ms. Murphy. With loving fondness, Sergeant Clayton Santos-Anderson," is what he had the woman at the shop write on the card. He asked the florist to deliver them to the public defender's office.

Two days later a thank you note from Ms. Murphy came in the mail to him at the police department. It smelled of lilacs and cinnamon. The card was made of a heavy paper and monogrammed with her initials. She had written, "Thank you for your many kindnesses. Iris Murphy."

Clayton wanted to call Ms. Murphy, but he did not. Nor did Ms. Murphy call him. But their encounter left him with a new found confidence. He wanted to waste no more time in his life. When doors opened he promised himself that he would enter rather than hesitate.

There was a new player on his slow pitch softball team and Clayton was attracted to her from their very first meeting. Her name was Claire Swenson. She worked at Millard North High School where she taught English language arts. Claire was from Roseville, Minnesota and had played first base on the softball team at Mankato State. Three days after his evening with Ms. Murphy, Clayton called Claire and asked her out for coffee the following Sunday. She said yes.

Claire met him after church at the Scooter's Coffee in Rockbrook Village. The shop was packed, so they took their drinks outside. They found an isolated table on the far side of the shopping plaza where they were alone.

"I always wanted my life to be like a Jane Austen novel," was the first thing that Claire said to him. "You know, witty conversation, misunderstanding, and then romance."

"Has it been?"

"Not at all."

"Are you sorry about that?"

"At times, I have been, but not now."

"How so?"

"Clayton, I'm thirty-seven-years old. I want a baby and I would like a husband."

"Wow," he remembers saying and then grinning.

"That's my Match.com version of Jane Austen and that's what I have to say to you today."

For a moment he stared at her. Claire Swenson was tall, blonde, and pretty. The kind of girl he always wanted in high school because he is a Minnesota boy. That kind of girl always felt unobtainable to him then, as a big, half-Mexican kid.

"I'm a divorced cop with a daughter in college. My first wife hated having to work outside the home. She hated my salary. We disagreed about the value of material things. She felt I lacked aspiration."

"This is the thing," Claire said, pushing back a strand of her blonde hair. "I really like you, but I don't have time to waste. If you don't want to be a father again and if you have given up on the idea of marriage then you're not the man for me. I cannot go on a second date with you unless I know that you want what I want."

Clayton grew very quiet and then said,

"I haven't given up on the idea of marriage, but I haven't done a lot of dating since my divorce. I always wanted another baby, but I'm closer to fifty than forty."

"I don't want a long courtship."

"Do you want to go to a movie on Friday night, then?"

"Sure."

They saw "Argo" and they both liked it. They ate popcorn. Clayton held Claire's hand. At the end of the evening, she kissed him on the cheek at the door of her townhouse.

"Would you like to have dinner here tomorrow night?" She asked him, looking over her shoulder and into the entryway.

"At your place?"

"Yes."

"Yes."

"Third date."

"The magic number," Clayton said, walking backwards to his truck. And she smiled.

Claire grilled steaks and Clayton brought the red wine. After dinner she put her grandfather's Nat King Cole albums on a record player and they danced in her living room cheek-to-cheek by candlelight. They continued to dance until the candles sputtered out and then Clayton began to kiss her, everywhere. Claire led him to her bedroom.

In the doorway, she said, "I'm not using birth control."

For a moment, Clayton pondered the condoms in his wallet and the many years of his divorced life. How solitary alone can feel. How much he had wanted other children and how long he had dreamed of reconciling with Darla. Then he picked up Claire Swenson and carried her over the threshold. She was not a bird. He unzipped her sundress and saw the map of Minnesota in her full breasts, sturdy hips, and flat extension of her stomach. He stripped off his clothes and she pulled him onto the bed.

"Let's make a baby," he whispered into her ear.

When Clayton Santos-Anderson came inside of Claire Swenson he saw a yellow bird fly across the room. It was then that he thought of Ms. Murphy. The bird hovered over them. His heart pounded. Claire held him against her substantial breasts, her legs wrapped around Clayton's back while she shuddered through a series of orgasms. When her wave subsided, Clayton asked her,

"Claire, will you marry me?"

She kissed him.

Clayton felt persistent. He wanted an answer.

"I love you, Claire. Will you marry me?"

"Well …" she said.

For a moment, Clayton panicked. What if she only wanted his sperm? This did happen to men and he didn't want it to happen to him. Even as he held her, he could imagine waking up next to Claire Swenson every morning and slow dancing with her every night after dinner. He wanted to be this woman's husband. Moreover he was certain his aim had been true. Cells were now dividing and molecules multiplying somewhere in one of Claire Swenson's fallopian tubes and moving to-wards her uterus. Clayton wanted this fragile bundle of being to be his as much as hers.

The bird began to flutter some kind of signal to him. So Clayton kissed Claire on the cheek and down her neck and she began to sigh and then he remembered that in high school he had memorized short poems for his first girlfriend and the girl had fallen in love with him.

"I dwell in possibility,'" he whispered to Claire, pulling her close.

The yellow bird landed on his shoulder, its tiny claws piercing his skin.

"Emily Dickinson," Claire cooed to him and he recited it all, loving the phrase, "And for an everlasting Roof/The Gambrels of the Sky-"

Claire began to nuzzle him and he whispered,

"'This Is Just To Say/I have eaten the plums that were in the ice-box and which you were probably saving for breakfast/Forgive me they were delicious so sweet and so cold.'"

"William Carlos Williams," she said, spreading her legs wide be-low him. "And I will marry you soon enough."

"I love you, Claire Swenson."

"I know," she said.

How do they always know, Clayton thought, but he did not say this to Claire, because he was inside of her, ready to memorize and recite a thousand poems to her for that privilege to continue.

The bird of his heart fluttered away.

In the morning, he found the yellow feather in Claire's bed. Four and a half weeks later, as they were driving home from softball practice, she said, "I'm pregnant."

"Sweet," Clayton said, grinning.

"I love you, Clayton Santos-Anderson, and I have loved you from the very moment I saw you on the softball field."

"Do tell," he said reaching for her thigh on the other side of the gearshift and squeezing it.

"Truly."

"Will you marry me, Claire?"

"Of course."

They set the date for Labor Day weekend. They are getting married in Roseville and Clayton's brother will officiate. Maria will be there. After the wedding they will go to the Minnesota State Fair.

All of this story he wants to tell to Ms. Murphy in Mark's Bistro. Making out with the public defender ripped open his staid and steady heart. Never would he have approached Claire without that night with Ms. Murphy. All these good turns in his life are because of her. It is apparent to Clayton that Iris Murphy has spent her time on earth giving more than she has ever gotten. But he tells her nothing. Between them at lunch is an invisible, but polite scrim. They eat their respective lunches and talk the business of police work and about the kind of clients Ms. Murphy represents. He tells her about his search for the mustard colored Mercedes Benz. When they have finished their food Clayton pays the bill. They leave together, his story untold.

In the cab of his truck, Ms. Murphy reaches for the paperback book that Clayton has tucked into the passenger door pocket. She turns the mauve-colored book over and reads aloud the title.

"*Love Poems* by Pablo Neruda."

"Yes, they are, love poems by Pablo Neruda."

And then Clayton starts the F150. He puts the truck into gear and slowly drives the three blocks to her house.

"You're in love with someone, Sergeant Santos-Anderson, and not with me."

"I will always be in love with you, Ms. Murphy," and even as he says the words he feels defensive. They are not exactly true, but they are true. He will always carry with him that night with Ms. Murphy that led to him to Claire. With Claire, Clayton is deeply, madly, truly in love.

"That's what all my boyfriends used to say to me when they were bidding me *adieu*."

"I'm not saying goodbye to you."

"You're blushing, Sergeant."

Clayton is embarrassed by the fact that Ms. Murphy found his book of love poems. He is memorizing Pablo Neruda's poems for Claire. He can feel his own defensiveness. All that he wanted to tell her about Claire now seems wrong, in bad taste. Ms. Murphy is still beautiful, but she seems frailer, and older, than she did on that night. Darkness softens everything, he thinks.

Then she says,

"I have stopped oncology."

"Why? People don't just stop oncology, Ms. Murphy."

"It made me sick. I didn't enjoy my living."

"But it will buy you time."

"But I won't enjoy that time. I will just be very sick and live only a little longer, if that."

"But …" is all Clayton can think to say

Now Clayton feels that this is goodbye.

Then Iris Murphy cuts to the chase. That's what all the cops say about her. She never wastes time in a courtroom unless there's great chance of winning for her clients. And that she hates prisons, or at least that's the rumor.

"I enjoyed kissing you, Sergeant Santos-Anderson. It made me realize that I wanted some semblance of a sexual life in what time I have. That night with you reminded me of my feelings on the topic."

"Well," he says as he parks his truck on her driveway. "It was a very special night for me as well."

Ms. Murphy is telling the story he wanted to tell.

"I want a loving, sexual relationship before I die."

"Well, you see, Ms. Murphy…"

"But not with you, Sergeant Santos-Anderson. So I'm glad that you're in love with someone else," she says, looking down at the book in her lap.

He blinks, deflated.

A vision of Claire comes over him and the child growing in her womb. He knows he has so much. It is a high school reaction, but he hates the feeling of being of dumped, even if it is by an older, dying woman. "Don't be petty, Clayton," he can hear his mother saying to him. Yolanda Santos-Anderson hates pettiness. Clayton knows he needs to call his mother.

"And I want to see my son, Miles, get married. And, of course, I want to vote in the presidential election."

Then he and Ms. Murphy look out the windshield of his truck at the Obama/Biden 2012 sign in the corner of her front yard. He does not remember seeing it on the evening that he brought Ms. Murphy home, but his mind was not on politics then. Drivers from three directions can see the words from two blocks away; it is that large. It is a sign that will piss off many Omahans, but not necessarily Ms. Murphy's neighbors. She lives in a blue sliver of a red state.

"I'll take a look around your house," he says, turning off the truck.

"Thank you, Sergeant Santos-Anderson," Ms. Murphy says.

Clayton helps her out of the cab. Ms. Murphy goes to stand by the Obama sign while he checks her house for security issues. Purple double-blooming petunias border the sign, as though it is a permanent edifice. He sighs. Political statements scream to the world, "Deface me" and they end up in the office of Property Crime.

He finds nothing to report. The home has been well maintained and her locks are sturdy, but sensible. She is the daughter of a firefighter and the building reflects this. The dog begins to bark from inside the house.

"Ferragamo has noticed you," she says.

"Everything looks fine."

"Thank you, Sergeant Santos-Anderson."

"But, if you have any worries, call me."

Ms. Murphy reaches for his hand.

"Sergeant Santos-Anderson, you and I are alike, you know."

"How so?"

"We love our jobs," she pauses, looking around the yard. "And we love others. Having love and work are life's greatest blessings."

Clayton nods his head.

"Is that the Mercedes you've been looking for?"

He sees it. A mustard colored vintage Mercedes Benz driven by an elegant woman rumbles down the street that fronts Ms. Murphy's side yard. One boy is in the front passenger seat and two boys are in the backseat with a covered birdcage between them.

"Please tell that woman it's a bad thing to teach children to steal from others, even if she needs the money. Stealing as a habit becomes imprinted on children as though they are ducklings. Also tell her I would like my money back, but I'm sure that it's long gone."

Clayton drops her hand.

"Ms. Murphy, you need to report crimes to the police when they happen. Not reporting breaks the social contract of a neighborhood. It leaves others vulnerable. You should know all this. You're a public defender."

Ms. Murphy blushes.

"I am so, so sorry, Sergeant Santos-Anderson."

Iris Murphy looks bereft and Clayton feels himself to be on higher moral ground, at least for the moment. For him, it is an emotional tit for tat. He gives her a grim look and nods his head.

"I've got to go."

Then he runs to his truck as a woman on a bicycle with a wicker basket pedals up the street to Ms. Murphy's house. She puts down the kickstand of her bike and walks over to Ms. Murphy. Clayton backs his truck into the empty street in pursuit of the Mercedes. In his rear view mirror, he sees Iris Murphy kiss her guest's lips and the woman respond in kind. They wrap their arms around each other. Together they stand next to the Obama/Biden sign watching his truck speed away as he watches them.

"Who are they hurting?" he says to the image of Pablo Neruda, looking up at him from the passenger seat. "Just tell me who could be hurt by their love?"

But Neruda is silent.

"Sex is the awkward made beautiful, Pablo, when there is love."

The poet does not respond.

Clayton shifts his gaze to the street and to what is ahead of him, the Mercedes, Claire, and their baby.

The Angel of Death
Smokes Cigarettes

THE TAXI STOPS IN FRONT OF HIS MOTHER'S HOUSE. There is a line of people leading up to the porch. Women in stocking caps and gloves who have bundled babies in their arms weave the infants back and forth as they slowly move forward. Men in suits and overcoats read folded newspapers. Guys wearing fake leather jackets and blue jeans smoke cigarettes. There are ponytails, Afros, and tattoos galore. Miles Murphy can see his uncle Walter working the front door. His aunt Bridget and Martha Berger are serving coffee from a card table near the Obama-Biden sign in the front yard. Lucy Spielman, a neighbor, is handing out cookies in plastic bags to the people queued up on the sidewalk.

"You know the lady who lives here?" The cabby asks him, looking through the windshield at the line into the red brick house.

"Yes," he says, handing the man forty dollars.

"She was in the paper. They called her a 'Friend to Felons.' Those are all crooks in that line. They've all come to say goodbye 'cause she's dying."

"She's my mother."

"I'm sorry," the cabby says, looking worried at the change in his hand.

"My mom was a public defender. Her father, my grandfather Jack served in World War II. He fought at Peleliu. Grandpa Jack was a deco-

177

rated Omaha fire fighter. I work for the State Department. All of us have been proud to serve our country."

"Here's your change."

"Keep the change."

"Thanks."

"The United States currently has more prisoners incarcerated than the Soviets ever did in their gulags. Many of them are serving sentences for petty amounts of drugs. They're young and they've made mistakes and they're poor. I'm sure you never smoked a joint in your life, but penitentiaries are very expensive punishments for non-violent crimes. My mom has spent her life making sure that poor people get due process."

Miles Murphy can hear the righteousness in his voice before it breaks. He sounds prissy in anger; it embarrasses him. But he is his mother's son. For a handful of seconds, he locks eyes with the cabby in the rear view mirror. And he thinks, but does not say, "You should be ashamed to say anything against my mom."

"I'll get your bags."

As the driver gets out of the taxi, Miles opens his door and steps into the cold December air. He slings his carry on bag over his shoulder and takes his suitcases from the man.

"Thank you," Miles says, as tears roll down his face.

The guy nods his head.

Miles walks to the Obama-Biden sign. It has been tagged, torn and then mended with colored duct tape. President Obama didn't take Nebraska, but he won his re-election and for his mom, Miles knows, this is enough.

His aunt Bridget leaves the table to wrap her arms around him. Miles drops his bags to the ground and returns the hug, kissing his aunt's soft gray curls. They rock back and forth.

Martha Berger looks at him with sad eyes.

"Oh, Miles, I'm so glad you're home."

"The cabby tells me that she made the newspaper."

"Well, it was either everyone gets to say goodbye or no one does," Martha says.

Over his aunt Bridget's head, he says, "So she chose everyone?"

Martha nods. "We had no idea. It's making Paul crazy."

Aunt Bridget releases him and signs, "Iris said that once you came home that she didn't want to see anyone else. This will be the last day. And soon the priest will need to come."

Miles nods his head. Mrs. Spielman brings him a cookie that he slips into his coat pocket. He kisses her cheek, and Mrs. Spielman says,

"Iris is waiting for you."

"Go to her," Aunt Bridget's hands say.

Miles picks up his bags and makes his way to the front door around the waiting people.

"Hey, Uncle Walter," he says.

"Come on in, Miles," Uncle Walter says, hugging him.

"The big Indian can't cut in line," someone shouts out from among the sad and restless group.

Miles turns around to face the people who are waiting to see his mother. He pushes his black eyeglasses up the bridge of his nose before he speaks.

"Hello everyone," he shouts out. "My name is Miles Murphy. I'm Ms. Murphy's son. Thank you for coming and thank you for your patience. I know my mom will want to see each one of you as soon as she can."

"It's her boy," a woman yells to the people in the crowd. "The kid in the pictures in her office."

Miles waves and then goes inside.

There in the front room is his mother in a hospital bed. Supported by pillows and dressed in a well-cut bed jacket, an emaciated Iris Murphy is listening to a man who is kneeling next to the bedrail. Beyond the scene at the bed Miles can see a nurse in one of his grandmother's Queen Anne chairs and his mom's friend, Paul Simmons, hovering like an angry bee. He can see his mom's big dog, Ferragamo, across from her at the fireplace. On the mantle of the fireplace Miles can see his grandmother's Christmas crèche and he can feel the tears begin again, but he blinks them away when he sees the dog watching him. Ferragamo looks concerned. Their attention is diverted when Iris Murphy speaks,

"Of course, of course," she says.

"Thank you for coming," Paul says to the man. "It's time to move on now."

A low rumble comes from deep within Ferragamo's chest.

The man stands up and the woman behind him goes to the side of the bed.

"Ms. Murphy, it's me, Destiny Branson."

"Destiny, how are you?"

"I've had my ups and downs, Ms. Murphy. But I've found Jesus. Nelly has sugar in his water, but other than that he's doing well in school."

"Give Nelly my love, Destiny."

"You will meet Jesus, Ms. Murphy."

"Thank you, Destiny. I hope so."

"God Bless you, that's what I want to say."

"God Bless you, Destiny."

"Have a good day, Destiny," Paul says and the woman circles back to Uncle Walter at the front door.

Miles waves to his mother. She waves back as he walks up the front stairs to put his luggage in his bedroom. There he pulls out his Black-Berry to call his wife in Nairobi.

Margaret asks him, "How is your mom?"

Miles shuts the door before describing the line and the hospital bed and the hospice nurse. Then he cries.

Margaret says, "I wish I could be there."

"No, you need to rest," he tells her before saying goodbye.

Seven hours later the last visitor leaves. His aunt and uncle and Paul and Martha all walk to Mark's Bistro for dinner. They will bring carry out for the nurse, Miles, and his mom. The house is quiet. Water rumbles through the radiators as the sun and the temperature go down.

The nurse reads on her Kindle while Miles watches his mother sleep. When he was seventeen, Miles can remember realizing what his birth meant to his mom, all that she had given up and all that she had sacrificed. It put him into a blue mood.

"I was the end of everything in your life."

"No, you were the beginning of everything in my life."

At the time his mom's words did not make him feel better and he began to argue with her. Every reasonable response she gave to his questions about his birth and his father, Cameron Kills Pretty Enemy, made him angry. The more heated he grew the more calm she seemed to be.

Finally he yelled, "Don't talk to me in that courtroom tone."

"Miles, your grandparents are in bed."

"You should have had an abortion. What kind of life is this? Living with your parents? Defending scum."

"Abortion is a private choice," she said to him. "You were my choice. I defend human beings, Miles Murphy, please, remember that."

And then his mother began to cry and said "I think I'll go to bed now."

Halfway up the stairs she called down to him, "I love you, Miles," as she always did, but for the next few days she was both chilly and functional in her mothering, definitely keeping her distance. And then it blew over, as everything does with Iris Murphy. His mother does not have the personality to hold a grudge, an important quality in a public defender. She believes in forgiveness. She lets things go.

Later in college he talked it all through in therapy, concluding with the words, "She wanted me. She always wanted me."

The therapist nodded her head.

"But she won't tell me anything about her relationship with Cameron Kills Pretty Enemy, except that she loved him. And somehow she thinks that's enough for me."

"Are you ever angry with your father?" The therapist asked him.

"I'm afraid to be angry with him because I'm afraid he would walk away from me like he did my mom. It's a power that he has over me. I'm afraid I'll lose him."

And this is still true.

The big dog moves closer to him. They both look at the sleeping woman. Miles puts his head in his hands. When he looks up he sees his mother watching him from her hospital bed.

"Miles," she says.

"Hey, Mom."

"How's my boy?"

"Well, I've had better days. That was quite a line out there. They tell me you made the *Omaha World Herald*."

"It must have been a slow news day."

"I don't think so, Mom."

"It's hard on people if they don't have a chance to say goodbye."

He nods his head and then says,

"Margaret sends her love."

"Your wife is beautiful. Knowing that she is your helpmeet makes everything easier for me."

"Helpmeet, Mom?"

"I wouldn't have minded a helpmeet, Miles."

"That's pretty old-fashioned term for a very modern woman to use."

"Modern for Omaha."

"Modern for anywhere in the world."

"I have loved my life."

"Do you have regrets?"

"I'm very sad that I will never meet my future grandchildren. I've always wanted to be a grandmother," she says this to him.

Then Miles begins to cry. The dog presses his muzzle into his hip.

His mother hands him a Kleenex from a box on the bed.

"Sweetie," she signs. "I need you to watch my hands."

It is what she would say to him when he was a little boy, when she had something important to tell him. The message was always in American Sign Language, Aunt Bridget's language.

His eyes turn to her hands.

"I want you to know this because I'm just not feeling very well and this may be the only time we have alone together. I have never been completely honest about how you came into the world, Miles, and now I must be. Your father and I had an ongoing affair. My time in the confessional cannot obliterate my shame for this, but there you have it. I knew that I could never be married to Cameron Kills Pretty Enemy, because he would not have left his wife. And honestly we had little in common, but our attraction to one another. But that did not stop me from being in love with him. Nonetheless, I wanted a baby and I planned you without telling Cameron. Then I broke up with him."

"Mom …"

"And then he found out …"

Her hands pause.

"Mom …"

"And Cameron was very unhappy with me … but I've written this all down for you. Uncle Paul will give it to you afterwards. I tried to answer every question I could imagine you might have."

"Mom."

"It was 1980, a very different time, trust me. Reagan was just elected. There were no single men left in Omaha, or at least none that were interested in me. I was in my early thirties and I felt like I was the oldest woman in the world and I wanted a baby."

"It's okay, Mom."

"I wanted to be a good mother more than anything else."

"You are."

"Without your grandparents I don't know what I would have done."

"I loved my childhood."

"Really?"

"Really," his hands say.

Then Iris Murphy begins to sob. The dog barks and the nurse puts down her Kindle and walks over to the bed,

"Iris, are you in pain?"

"A little."

"What is your number?"

"Seven."

"Seven is more than a little, Iris. Let me get some of my magic potions."

His mom nods her head.

Miles wipes his mother's face with a handkerchief that Margaret had given him. It is linen and from Ireland. He holds his mom's hand. The nurse adjusts the medications, checks his mother's vital signs, and walks into the kitchen for fresh water.

Then his mother says in a hoarse whisper to him, "I would have done all the chemotherapy, but I could smell the Angel of Death everywhere. He smokes cigarettes, you know. What's the use of losing all of your hair and having surgery when the Angel of Death is smoking Marlboros in your backyard? I knew the game was up and now I'm in the crucible."

"Mom, I don't think that…" but Miles stops because the nurse re-appears, as if on cue.

"It's the truth," she signs to him.

The truth is that it must be his mother's drugs, but he would never say this. The truth, at this point, does not matter.

"Would you please walk Ferragamo?"

"Sure," he says, smiling.

Miles loves to walk dogs.

As he stuffs the plastic bags into his coat pocket he finds the bag Mrs. Spielman had handed to him. In it is a sugar cookie cut in the shape of a holly wreath. It is frosted in an evergreen color and decorated with silver nonpareils. Miles eats it in two bites.

"Life is sweet, Ferragamo. No matter what," he tells the dog, as he opens the front door.

The night is clear and the stars are as bright as the Christmas lights strung throughout the neighborhood. Miles allows Ferragamo to lead him. The dog is a brisk walker, but he does not pull on the leash. He knows where he wants to stop and what he wants to sniff. The animal has elegant manners.

"Manners are far more important in a dog than pedigree," his grand-pa Jack used to say. "And in humans, too."

Dog walkers who see him as he passes under the streetlights call out,

"Hey, Miles, your mother's in our prayers."

Or, "Give Iris, my best."

Miles loves Dundee. Whenever he comes home it is as if he has never left. Some people have no idea that he lives and works in Nairobi. They are just glad to see him. But this time they know about his mom. Omaha, like all cities, is but a patchwork of neighborhoods.

On one of their first dates Margaret asked him, "Was it hard to be the only dark-skinned boy in your neighborhood? I mean because you didn't look like your mom, exactly. And isn't Nebraska very white?"

It is the kind of question that people of color will ask another person of color.

And Miles answered her with these words.

"I was a chubby little brown boy with thick glasses and people were kind to me and my mom. All the grown ups knew me in the neighborhood. When I was a toddler they saw me walking the dog with my grandfather. We were always walking the dog. My grandfather believed that a boy needed a dog."

In fourth grade his classmates noticed that he did not look like his mom and that his dad was not in the picture. They asked questions. Miles felt awkward. His mother's response was,

"Human beings notice differences, but they also notice similarities as well. We are created to be aware of our surroundings. My clients always get in trouble because they don't notice that other people notice. It's good to be aware of that reality, Miles. People are paying attention to you. It's not just God."

Miles cannot even conceive of being that direct with a nine-year-old, but his mother always was. His grandparents, he suspects, were equally blunt with their daughters. So his mom did not fall far from the tree in that respect. But his grandparents were very protective of him, and his cousin Ezra.

"Little boys are more tender than girls," he saw his grandmother sign to his aunt Bridget, thinking Miles and Ezra weren't looking. "We have to look out for them."

"Most definitely," his aunt's hands responded.

Miles is afraid that this is true, even of men.

"I'll speak to the boy's father," his grandfather once said, when he heard from a neighbor that a child was picking on Miles.

Grandpa Jack did speak and it ended the teasing immediately. It felt like magic to Miles. Miles is sure that it was not an intercession Jack

Murphy ever performed for his daughters when they lived on Webster Street. His mother and his aunt, he is sure, had to tough it out. He, on the other hand, grew up unafraid, walking the lovely streets of the Dundee neighborhood of Omaha with a dog at his side. Everyone waved to him and said "Hey Miles." He may have been a dark-skinned little boy, but he didn't think much about it. Except for a handful of bleak and private moments in his adolescence Miles swam in the shallow waters of happiness during his years in Nebraska. The experience has made him a very reasonable and kind man.

Foreign Service has taught Miles that there are many things that money can fix. It pains him when people refuse to use money to fix what can be mended. People die everyday because of this selfishness. But he also realizes there is so much that money cannot fix. He wonders if money could fix his mother and he worries that she gave up on oncology too soon. Without her he feels he will become an orphan. For as much as he has grown to love Cameron Kills Pretty Enemy, he knows that his true parent lies a few blocks away in a rented hospital bed, dying.

As he and Ferragamo walk into the 50th and Underwood business district, Miles turns his mind to Christmas. It is a season that he has always loved. Putting up the lights and decorating the tree were things that his grandparents enjoyed. He and his mom could both help, but still be children. Before he left Nairobi, he assembled a tree for Margaret.

"It's lovely," she said, from her position on the couch.

"I always want us to be happy at Christmas, no matter where we are in the world."

Margaret smiled.

"We will."

"Promise?"

"Girl Scout's honor."

He laughed.

"That's as good as a pinkie swear."

In second grade he was home with the chicken pox on Halloween night and he had to abandon his Batman costume for a long soak in an Aveeno oatmeal bath. He could hear the doorbell ringing and his grandparents greeting children in costume. And his mom, who was sitting on the side of the bathtub, asked him,

"What makes you happy, Miles?"

"Well, Halloween."

She smiled.

"Besides Halloween."

"Well, Christmas."

"How about Thanksgiving?"

"Well, if Nebraska wins the football game then I'm happy."

"So is your grandfather."

He giggled.

"What makes you happy on your way to school?"

"Thinking about science class and library time."

"Always think about what makes you happy when you're not feeling so good."

"Why?"

"Because it's like hope. It reminds you that things will get better."

"Ferragamo," Miles says aloud.

The dog stops. They are a block from the house.

"My mom is a very good woman."

Ferragamo looks at him and sits down.

"I know I didn't have to tell you that. But I want you to know that I know that."

The dog waits as Miles pauses.

"And Ezra and I will take care of you. That's the other thing."

The dog's jaw drops at the sound of the name "Ezra."

"We will."

Then Ferragamo leads Miles home.

There is a van on the driveway when they arrive.

His cousin Ezra opens the front door and Ferragamo begins to bark.

"Hey, Miles," his cousin says, grabbing him in a bear hug.

"Thanks for coming."

"They brought home enough food to feed an army."

Uncle Walter brings dining room chairs to the side of the hospital bed. Miles and Ezra sit on them. Aunt Bridget hands each of them a plate. Their conversation stops. The cousins eat. They are ravenous. The nurse, Paul and Martha and Ezra's mom and dad float in an out of the room like satellites. Conversations take place in library voices and American Sign Language while his mother sleeps.

Ferragamo barks when Iris Murphy awakens.

She speaks.

"Miles, will you take Ferragamo back to Nairobi with you? You know a boy always needs a dog."

"I think Ferragamo will go back to Cincinnati with Ezra, Mom."

"But Ezra's mean cat picks on the dog."

"Horace Mann is not mean, Aunt Iris."

The other conversations halt. Lips close and hands drop.

"Mom, it's just that I don't think Nairobi would be a good place for Ferragamo."

"Don't Kenyans keep pet dogs?"

"Of course, but my apartment is small."

"Does Margaret like dogs?"

"Well, she's never had one."

"So she doesn't like dogs?"

His mother asks this question with a note of concern in her voice. Not liking dogs in the Murphy family hints at a possible personality defect, or worse.

Miles hangs his head and sighs.

"Miles," she says.

"Mom, Margaret's pregnant."

"Why didn't you tell me?"

"I was going to do that soon enough. But the house was filled with people when I got home. It just wasn't the time."

All the eyes in the room turn on him.

"But, Miles …"

Everyone in the room can hear the tears in Iris Murphy's voice.

Ferragamo growls.

Ezra says, "Shush," to the dog.

"Margaret's at home. It's early in the pregnancy. She's been sick every day all day. The nausea makes it hard for her to eat. Margaret's mother flew over from Ithaca. She's with her now. The doctor thinks she's going to be okay, but it's been rough. Our apartment is no place for a dog right now."

The room is still. The clouds clear from his mother's eyes. The quiet looms and then she smiles.

"Miles, I'm going to be a grandmother."

"Yes, Mom."

"Martha, did you hear that?"

"Yes, Iris, darling. Congratulations."

Then everyone says, "Congratulations!"

They break out some Coca Colas and 7Ups and his grandmother's Waterford crystal. They toast the future Murphy. The talk is happy. It feels like Christmas to Miles.

"Iris Murphy will be the most gorgeous grandmother in the world," Paul Simmons says to the group around the hospital bed.

It is then that Miles hears the scratching sound of a wooden match being struck and the small burst of its flame. He is startled when he smells the cigarette smoke wafting through the room. Trying to quit smoking was a central theme of adult conversation in his boyhood. No one in this room has smoked for years.

Miles scans the room. The nurse is smiling and Aunt Bridget is suggesting names for the baby to Ezra in sign language.

"It has been a dream of mine to visit Africa and now there is a reason," Uncle Walter tells Uncle Paul. "Bridget and I will go to see the baby."

Martha Berger is brushing his mother's silver hair.

No one else smells it. He looks into his mom's eyes. Her hands call out to him.

Miles goes to the side of the hospital bed. Sitting down he leans into his mother, as Martha Berger steps back. His mom puts her warm hands on his cheeks, pushing his glasses askew. She pulls him forward and looks into his eyes.

People stop talking. Fingers rest in laps. Mother and son have become the pieta in their midst.

Miles peers into his mother's blue-gray eyes. Cigarette smoke swirls around the two of them. Inside of it, they are alone. He feels the breath-taking pain of her dying as she holds him there with her hands and her eyes. Part of him wants to follow her and he can feel her pushing him back into the world, the universal tug of war that is mother and child. Miles Murphy aches. His heart feels scratched.

The nurse leaves the room.

"Your baby … " his mother whispers to him in a panting rasp.

Her eyes widen.

"Yes, Mom," he says, his hands now on top of hers. Sweat and tears pour down his face and snot runs from his nose.

"Forward," she whispers to him.

"Where are we going?" he would ask her on the weekends of his boyhood.

"Grocery shopping, Target, the usual," she'd say.

"But aren't we going somewhere?"

Miles Murphy always wanted to go somewhere — a ballgame, a

movie, a park, on vacation.

"While the earth is spinning on its axis we're going forward," is how she would answer him.

"To where?" he would then ask her.

"To tomorrow."

Seized up by the pain, Iris Murphy closes her eyes. The nurse returns with medication. Ferragamo begins to howl.

Ezra moves to comfort Ferragamo as Miles whispers into his mother's ear, "The earth is spinning on its axis."

"Forward," her hands sign.

Acknowledgments

I want to thank Janet Wiehe and Marie Stolte, my faithful readers of many years. Also I need to acknowledge Theresa Farrell-Strauss of the Hennepin County Attorney's Office who has patiently explained details of the law to me over the many years that I have been asking her questions, to her many thanks. And to Lynne Morishita who explained medical procedures to me. To Jim Roth, beekeeper and friend, believer in my writing, has kept me fortified with great honey for years. Thanks as well to Lily Baber Coyle for telling me a story about a political yard sign. Thanks as well to Lorraine Langdon-Hull, Sheila O'Connor, Deb Nelson, Johanna Buch, Lynne Stanley, and Baxter Nelson.

The staff and patrons of the Edina Library and the Friends of the Edina Library have greatly enriched my life with their kindness and moral support and to them thanks are due. In particular, I need to thank Mr. James Tarsney who checks in on my writing career on a weekly basis. He has great faith in me and in so many people in the world. Mr. Tarsney is a wonderful human being who does kind deeds daily to make the world a better place.

I also want to thank Jill Vuchetich, Barb Economon, Martha Ruddy, Dr. Michael Peterman, and Peter Murphy of the Walker Art Center and its Library and Archives. Thank you for the gift of filing catalogue cards. It is very good for the soul.

Thank you to my husband, Dan, and daughter, Kerry, my brother, Tim, my sisters, Joan, Megan, and Kathleen, and to my many friends and family.

Many thanks to Joe Taylor, and the Livingston Press of the University of West Alabama. God Bless the spirit of Ruby Pickens Tartt, a great woman.

Finally to those who have passed, Marty Wright, Rosemary Furtak, Mark Cole, Scott Belkin, William Francis Millea, and Dr. Daniel Newton Smith, Jr., I miss you all.

Maureen Millea Smith is the author of *When Charlotte Comes Home,* which won the Minnesota Book Award for Novel & Short Story in 2007. Her essay "In Charlotte's Web" was published in Minnesota Literature in December 2003 and was chosen as the winner of the 2003 Minnesota Literature essay contest.

She has an MFA in Creative Writing from Hamline University and an MA in Library Science from the University of Iowa. Her undergraduate degree is from the University of Wyoming in English Literature. She presently works as a reference librarian and readers' advisor at the Edina Library of the Hennepin County Library system. At the Edina Library, she works on author programs, including the Edina Reads series, the Loft First Pages Labs, and the Great Decisions programs in collaboration with speakers from the Minnesota International Center. She worked for the Public Library of Cincinnati and Hamilton County for eleven and one-half years, seven of which were in the Fiction and Young Adult Department.

She lives in Edina with her husband and a Maine Coon cat named Winnie and a rescue cat name Schubert Shed Cat IV. Their daughter is a violist and is in graduate school at College Conservatory of Music at the University of Cincinnati in arts administration.